MW00908929

WITHDRAWN
FROM COLLECTION
VPL

Evening Light

Harold Horwood

Pottersfield Press
Lawrencetown Beach, Nova Scotia, Canada

Canadian Cataloguing in Publication Data

Horwood, Harold, 1923–

Evening Light
ISBN 1-895900-06-9

I. Title.
PS8515.074E83 1997 C813'.54 C97-950014-1
PR9199.3.H5954E83 1997

Cover photographs by Andrew Horwood

Acknowledgements: Short episodes from this book have been published in the following journals: *The New Quarterly*, *The Fiddlehead*, *Canadian Fiction Magazine*, and *Pottersfield Portfolio*.

Pottersfield Press gratefully acknowledges the ongoing support of the Nova Scotia Department of Education, Cultural Affairs Division, as well as the Canada Council and the Department of Canadian Heritage.

Printed and bound in Canada

Pottersfield Press
Lawrencetown Beach
83 Leslie Road, East Lawrencetown
Nova Scotia, Canada, B2Z 1P8

In memory of
my friend, neighbour, and colleague
Bill Percy

CONTENTS

A Shaft of Sun, a Wisp of Cloud

Small pools of sunlight, spots of gold on the hard, brown surface of the kitchen floor — Jonathan doesn't know the word "linoleum" though he must have heard it pronounced now and then by his elders — the sunlight moving, dancing. Looking up, he understands that the dancing lights are shaped by curtains blowing in the breeze, but most of what he sees and feels as he crawls on the floor he accepts without explanation. The universe still runs on magic. Beams falling through dust motes, shining like paths in the air, petals drifting through the window — none of this appears to have a cause, only a being.

Sting of a switch on his bottom as his mother stands over him, sharp, shocking, her voice scolding, angry. Jonathan's own voice rising in a wail, knowing that a crying tantrum is the one sure way to punish her. Then, afterwards, being hugged, and sinking into sleep.

Outside — grass, moss, twigs tickling his feet, making his toes curl. He is still unsteady as he walks upright with his father's help. He watches a bumble bee, large, furry, benign, its head buried in a blossom. While his father holds him he reaches out a finger and touches the bee's fur very, very gently. The bee is not disturbed. Perhaps it is used to the touch of a petal, or a leaf. What is it doing? From some place unimaginable the word comes to him — has his father said it? "It's pollinating the flowers" he thinks, seeing the bee as serving the plants, performing its assigned task in the work of the world.

Strawberries. Red. Very scented. They hang by ones and twos, hidden beneath the leaves. You must crouch right down to find them, or better, crawl on your belly, feeling the plants prickling your skin, smelling the scent, stuffing the berries into your mouth, green leaves getting in there too by accident, the juice trickling down your chin — no matter; his father will wash him off later.

Black currants shining like beads among bright leaves. A few of the leaves are rolled into tight curls. Pick them apart. Inside is white wool, and a tiny green worm that has made a home there for itself. Eat the worm? No, he knows already that worms aren't for eating. Spit bugs, hiding in blobs of spit on green stems. Rub the spit between your fingers, and there is the bug, as green as a new-shelled pea.

This must have been early summer, but there are other images from another part of that eternal year:

Cabbages, hard and white, green leaves picked off and left in the garden, each head wrapped in newspaper and taken to the cellar. By now he can comment on what he seas in abbreviated sentences: Cabbages like footballs. He has seen older boys kicking a ball around a grassy lot, and others chasing an inflated bladder in their bare feet. Later, he knows, the cabbages will be boiled with salt pork in a pot, perhaps with pease pudding too, the pot liquor salty, the cabbage dripping fat, long orange fingers of carrots lying beside it on the platter, with round knobs of potatoes.

Eat your vegetables they're good for you they'll make you grow — advice from the world of giants with which he is surrounded.

Running, tripping, falling, a tiny spot of blood, tears, wails, protest against ... against what? ... the unfairness, as he sees it, of things-as-they-are.

Early morning, the air cold, cold, feathers of frost on the kitchen window. You can make a spot with your thumb and peer through it, or better yet, breathe a clear hole with warm breath, a tiny porthole covered with clear wavy ice that makes waves and wrinkles in the world outside. Standing in front of the kitchen range, where his father has lit the fire, pyjamas in a heap on the floor, spots of bright warmth from the grate playing over his body, feeling really good in the cold air, stroking like gentles fingers. Soon porridge will be steaming on the back of the stove, and his mother will arrive with his clothes, demanding that he get dressed. He's learning to do it, to put his shorts on right-side-front, turn socks inside out to make them easier to pull over his heels. Shoes, of course, will be on the wrong feet. And shirt buttons are still a problem. Will he ever get them right? As for outdoor clothes, there's a bewildering array of the stuff — jackets, scarves, wool caps double-knitted mitts, boots that must be tied at the top — all of it soaking wet when you come back in. They hang it to dry behind the range while you sit at the open oven door soaking up the heat, flames dancing like red-jacket elves through the joints of the range.

Another morning. Still mid-winter. This time no frost on the pane. The sun is shining, and the world outside has turned to pure fantasy, the palace and gardens of the Ice Queen. In the night there has been a glitter storm — his grandmother calls it a silver thaw — and every twig and wire and tuft of spruce is dancing with light; your eyes are dazzled with sunbeams shooting in every direction from trees and shrubs that only yesterday were drab-brown and black. What snow remains on the ground will be crusted with the silver thaw, and sleds will go rocketing downhill at breakneck speeds.

Spring again. Horses pulling carriages, carts, heavy loads on "slovens" as his grandfather calls them — flat-bedded, iron-wheeled freight carriers pulled by teams of huge animals. Jonathan, still not old enough to wander abroad by himself, stands at the gate watching the big draught horses sweating under the drovers' whips, the smart, slender-legged carriage horses jumping and switching their tails as the bright yellow buggy whips crack around their rumps. Fascinated, aroused by the whips, he doesn't wonder about it at the time; it is just something that happens. He'll wonder about it later, though much later, when his urges become conscious, and he begins suppressing the excitement he feels at cruelty, one of the unworthy tendencies within himself, wondering where it came from, wondering why in some strange way it is associated with pools of sunlight on linoleum.

Going with Mother on visits, just able to keep up, his short legs making three steps to her one. Old ladies they visit, offer him cookies or candies. They talk, talk, talk — incomprehensible talk, while he wonders about the strange ornaments on their mantle shelves, and the fantastic iron figures dancing around their fireplaces. Gazing through panes of coloured glass above their windows and doors, he sees the world transformed into something alien and joyful.

A bit later. Holding his grandfather's hand, gazing at ships being built on the stocks, all ribs and beams, the sky shining through, a wonderful thing to see, a ship coming to birth, spokeshaves and draw-knives taking paper-thin shavings from parts that must fit exactly, the master shipwright, to whom his grandfather speaks with respect, almost as an equal, running the long wooden jackplane over a timber.

"Keelson," he explains, "fer that new one jest starting over there."

"Not much shipbuilding here any more," his grandfather says to the shipwright.

"No Captain. Not like it was in me father's time. Used to launch a dozen new ships a year, I 'low .... Over in Trinity, now, there's still three yards building fishing ships."

"Aye. So I hear. They've been buildin' ships there fer nigh on three hundred year."

"A sad thing, Captain, if it dies out. Looks like we'll be down to punts and trap skiffs pretty soon."

"Yes. I s'pose so."

Next to the shipyard, the forge. Blacksmith with a sledgehammer pounding great showers of yellow and red sparks like shooting stars from white-hot metal on the anvil. You must keep well back while you watch. The bellows puff into the bed of coals, making blue flames hiss above the forge, and fire go roaring up the flue. Hot metal from the anvil is tossed into a puncheon tub of water, and clouds of steam wrap the blacksmith like fog.

Greatest wonder of all, perhaps: a *five*-masted ship, tied up to the pier, a huge, wind-driven freighter.

"Built in Europe," his grandfather tells him. "Maybe the only time ye'll ever see the like, Johnnie. Nobody on this side o' the Western Ocean is building ships like that any more."

Jamie Penchley and himself taking turns pushing each other on the swing because they're still not big enough to "work up" to its full height. Taking turns jumping off the swing as it rises, flying out in a slow arc, upwards at first, then down in a curve to the soft grass, landing safely on all fours, flying. Better not let Mother catch you, or she'll yell blue murder and send you home to stand in the corner.

Chasing a hoop along the road, using a short stick to guide it and keep it rolling. Most boys have barrel hoops, or hoops from puncheon tubs, but Jonathan has a great treasure, an iron band from a cart wheel, standing as high as his head. It is all he can do to control it, to keep it from escaping and running wild, for it has a life of its own, always fighting against his control.

He and Jamie on the edge of the barrens, where the cliff falls into the bushes far below. Here there is a great rock balanced on a sheet of flat stone, looking as if it might fall at the merest touch. They stand behind the rock, and push with all their might. It refuses to budge. Oh well — perhaps when they are bigger. They do not know that generations of boys have been trying for centuries to push that rock over the edge.

His Uncle Sid helping him to tie a "cast" for trout — two wet flies a foot or so apart, followed by a "tail bait" — a worm on a hook. Trout chases the flies. Sees the worm. Grabs it. Then bingo! you've got him. He's still too young to cast for trout, but not too young to trail the line downstream in a brook, and haul a wriggling eight-inch fish ashore among the willows. That trout, his first, will never be forgotten, though a thousand others may follow it to the frying pan, and the place he caught it will be an enchanted place forever — a wooden bridge, a small tumbling rapids, a couple of black rocks standing above the water, and a quiet pool below.

Playing with Jamie and other boys on the open square in front of the Catholic church. Catholics and Protestants are tolerant in this town, have always been friendly. There is none of the religious rioting that once disgraced Carbonear and Harbour Grace and even St. John's. Nuns teach music to Protestant children. The Orange band plays in the St. Patrick's Day parade.

He and Jamie run up the stone steps of the church and into the candle-lit interior. It is darker, more beautiful than the churches he sometimes attends with his mother; more hushed, more sacred. The marble floor feels deliciously cool — barefoot children are welcome in this imposing church, can play on its steps, even in its nave. If they tried it in a Protestant church they'd quickly be shooed outside. Protestant churches are kept locked up, anyway, except on Sundays, or at weddings and funerals.

Jonathan shyly approaches the altar. Candles glimmer like red stars in the dimness, shining through glass beside the skirts of stone saints. He feels a sense of awe as he approaches the altar, quiet as a mouse. A woman is kneeling there, wearing the habit of a nun, a rosary hanging at her waist. She becomes aware of his presence, looks at him and smiles then picks him up and sits him on the altar rail.

"How beautiful you are!" she says, "like one of the children in the Bible — the boy Samuel, perhaps, who lived in the House of the Lord, wearing the linen ephod of a priest. Do you know what an ephod is, my child?"

Speechless, he shakes his head.

"It is a simple white shift without sleeves, open below the arms, and tied with a girdle. Samuel's mother made such garments for her child to wear in the House of the Lord, and once a year she also made him a little coat."

The nun takes the boy's feet in her hands and kisses them, then sets him back upon the floor and kisses his forehead. "Run along and play," she says. "Our Lord loves you, as He loved the children in Palestine." The scent of lavender from her garments mingles with the scent of hot wax from the candles before the altar, creating a spell of sanctity.

Outside in the hot sunshine Jonathan is a bit awed by it all, but Jamie thinks it is nothing special, and dismisses it with a worldly shrug.

"That's Sister Marie of Gethsemane," he says. "You're lucky she didn't take you around the Stations of the Cross and stop to say a prayer at each one."

"That wouldn't be so bad," Jonathan says. "Maybe she'll do that another day."

"Well, don't let on about it at home, is all, or you're liable to be put on bread and water for a week."

"Why?"

"Oh ... you know ... Popish stuff!"

So the world still runs on magic, but the magic recedes, becomes more and more distant as he grows older. It vanishes into a wisp of cloud on his first day at school.

Taurus

Paddy Lewis's red bull went snorting and plunging along the fence line looking for a way to break out of the field where juniper posts, spruce longers, and barbed wire combined to imprison him. Jersey bulls had a bad reputation. Boys were cautioned not to tease them; you might get away with teasing a horse, a gander, or even a billy goat, but a Jersey bull would just as soon kill you as look at you. Paddy Lewis's bull had been known to break out, and range up and down the main road looking for someone to gore with his long, viciously sharp horns, while women rushed indoors and children cowered behind fences.

Jonathan's father, though, wasn't afraid of bulls. He took heifers to visit the bull when the heifers came into heat, and stood there unafraid while the bull came foaming up to the young cow, and the animals performed their ugly parody of what some people called "making love." There was no trace of love in the heart of a bull, that was for sure, just unalloyed savagery, but Jonathan's father declared that even a bull wouldn't face a good-sized rock, about as big as a goose egg, hurled determinedly at the spot between his eyes. Jonathan's father knew what he was talking about, because he had driven the beast off with just such a missile when it was snorting and pawing the ground, and getting ready to charge.

Jonathan hefted the rock in his hand and decided against it. Maybe the rock would drive the monster off. Maybe it would just make him mad enough to break down the fence. He decided instead that if the beast did get out he'd be able to vault over the fence himself, and be safe on the other side. He had a vision of vaulting back and forth as the bull broke through the fence time and again in pursuit of him, the two of them zigzaging down the fence line, barefoot boy and bellowing bull turning Paddy Lewis's fence into a tangle of broken longers and barbed wire. He laughed aloud.

At the sound the bull stopped snorting and glared at him. And suddenly between himself and the bull there was a current flowing — not any kind of fellow-feeling like you might have with a dog — nothing like that; the bull was still his enemy, supremely dangerous — but suddenly he seemed to see the world through those malevolent jet-black eyes, feel it through those wicked jet-black hooves, a world where all was enmity, and opposed to the enmity was nothing except a tremendous package of naked power, bull against the universe, poised for total destruction.

He shuddered, had a fleeting glimpse of blackness, and then it passed. But the bull walked away, his fury dying. Perhaps the bull, too, had glimpsed something in that brief moment of confrontation, that strange electric flash that had come and gone so quickly.

Jonathan walked off, tossing the stone aside, feeling demeaned that he had ever picked it up. What was it his grandfather had told him? Bulls had been worshipped in the days of long ago, by the Egyptians, by the Assyrians, by the Babylonians, by the Hebrews. Why would people worship a bull? He pondered for a minute, then thought of an answer. They were worshipping power — that might be it — worshipping what they most feared... But perhaps there was more to it than that? Had someone back then glimpsed the world through the eyes of a bull?

Jonathan went looking for his grandfather, and found the old captain working over a chart, with pencil, dividers, and parallel rule. When he tried to tell him what had happened up at Lewis's meadow, Captain Josh chuckled with amusement:

"Ye are a funny lad. Perhaps it all happened in yer own head. Have ye thought o' that?"

"No sir. I don't think so."

The captain grunted. "Well ... let's see ... the Indians might have called the bull your totem."

"What does that mean, sir?"

"A totem is a kind of animal spirit that takes care of you — becomes a guide. Were ye an Indian, perhaps ye'd take the name Red Bull." The old man laughed again. "Ye'd like that?"

"No sir ... and besides," he grinned, enjoying the joke, "I wouldn't want Paddy Lewis's bull following me around, even as a spirit."

"No, I s'pose not ... Did ye know that bulls were connected with the sea? Many a ship had a bull's face, or a pair o' horns fer a figurehead. Back when Moses was in Egypt they put bulls' heads on the points o' their prows. Greeks did it too, with their warships. An' later on the Vikings — the fighting boats they called longships had dragon heads sometimes, an' sometimes the heads o' bulls."

"Why bulls?" Jonathan asked. "Dragons I understand ... or lions."

"The sea itself is a bull, sometimes," the captain told him, "an' the storm too, o' course. An' ships in those days used to charge an' ram one another, like fighting bulls."

That night in bed, as he drifted toward sleep, Jonathan lay thinking of what his grandfather had said ... something about "the bull of heaven" and "the great bull of the sea." Britain was a bull, he remembered — John Bull — but it didn't seem to fit very well. He couldn't think of Britain as naked power defying implacable enemies, though perhaps it was like that back in Napoleon's time, a time his grandfather's grandfather would have known. He thought about the march of generations, a parade of boys walking through a vague landscape turning very slowly into old men as they walked. And then there was ... there is ... this spirit face, all mist and silver, coming out of a cloud, a face and a voice, "Thou art my beloved son ..." It changed and melted, as it always did, and he was on a plain with banners going by.

Jonathan's dreams never seemed to follow along from what he had been thinking about before sleep. If there was a connection, it was too deep for him to fathom. And he was never much good at remembering dreams. They passed into a wandering mist, beyond recall. He believed they still existed, somewhere, though he couldn't reach them, like a book in a foreign language that no one could read.

Next morning he went back to the fence on the high meadow to look at the bull, but he was unable to recapture anything from the day before. There would be no returning to the moment of revelation, and he began to wonder if, after all, anything had really happened in that electric moment. Perhaps, as the captain had suggested, it was all in his own head. Anyway, the bull was off by himself in the middle of the field, grazing on red and white clover, totally uninterested in Jonathan or anyone else.

As Jonathan turned away, disappointed, Jamie Penchley came over the ridge from the harbour, flicking stones from a catapult, and actually hitting fence posts as he came. It must take weeks and months of practice to aim a stone like that.

"Hey Jonathan, wanna go up to the beaver pond swimming?"

"Yeah, sure. you think there'll be any beavers?"

"Guaranteed. Might be some young ones too, this time o' year."

"Say ... you don't aim to shoot at them with that catapult?"

"Hell no. My Dad'd skin me if I killed a young beaver ... Might take a shot at that old bull, though."

"Don't you dare!"

The boys walked off together, bulls and spirits soon forgotten, under the same sun that had shone upon Apis at a far distant time in a distant land.

The Pleasures of Drift Ice

Levi Johnston's sail loft was across the main road on the waterfront just opposite the wharves. At ground level Johnston's store was full of coils of rope, great hanks of knitting twine, single and double and even triple hardwood blocks with hooks for hanging them and spindles for reeving hoists, block and tackle as the men all called them. There were also deadeyes for mounting standing rigging, iron thole pins, and similar gear. All this stuff was for sale as well as for use in the trade, and was tended by a boy who served customers, swept and cleaned the store, and ran errands for Levi Johnston and his two tradesmen who presided upstairs where there was one big room with benches and shelves and stools and tubs for sitting, and floor space for laying out the sails, and sail needles and sail thread for the sailmakers.

The upper storey was a wonderful place, warm even in winter from the wood-burning heater with its supply of birch billets, and always smelling strongly of barked canvas and oakum. Sails were repaired here, as well as being made new to order, and now and then a tradesman stitched together a straitjacket for the jail over in Harbour Grace. The straitjacket might be used to restrain a lunatic until he could be transferred to the lunatic asylum in St. John's.

The loft was both a centre of industry and one of the main social centres of the town. It was here that the ships' captains and the fish inspector and the magistrate foregathered on winter afternoons to discuss the state of the world, the prospects for trade, and the wickedness of whatever government happened to be in power at the moment. Governments might come and go — they were especially liable to collapse during a budget debate — but their judges were always in session in Levi Johnston's sail loft.

Boys, sometimes brought there by grandfathers, were tolerated in this sanctum so long as they kept well out of the way, and spoke not a word except to say "yes, sir" if somebody asked them to go to the general store for a plug of Beaver pipe tobacco. Some of the elders who made regular visits to the sail loft smoked pipes; others regarded all tobacco as an invention of the devil, but in either case they would not have countenanced a cigarette smoker. At most he might have been admitted to the retail store down below — good enough place for him; cigarettes were for barbarians, soldiers, longshoremen or the like — and boys, it must be admitted, smoked cigarettes on the sly, rolling their own from finely-shaved pipe tobacco, nearly choking on the strong fumes, and with the likelihood of getting a licking if they were caught. Pipes were suitable for men of substance, but Jonathan's father and grandfather had never touched tobacco in their lives, and his Uncle Sid was considered something of a family disgrace because he had brought back a briar pipe from one of his foreign voyages. There were rumours that a few Irish women smoked at home, but such conduct was almost too disgraceful to mention. The air of the sail loft often carried the aroma of the evil weed, but was never really thick with it. Pipes went out the minute you laid them down; the smoke found its way to the stove and up the flue.

Jonathan learned lessons in politics, civics and foreign affairs while sitting out of the way in Levi Johnston's sail loft. It was there he learned how political assassinations in Brazil and revolutions in Spain could affect the price of fish, how the Tory Gang in St. John's were barely hanging on, while *The Evening Telegram* thundered for their instant dismissal, how the young men and women who had gone off to the Boston States were prospering, how the godless scientists were denying the Creation and saying men were descended from apes, how steamships were setting new Atlantic records that even the great clippers of a generation earlier could not have matched. As an institution of higher learning, no school could compare with the sail loft; it was the perfect place for a boy to be seen and not heard.

One sunny day in March when the ice was "in," with the bay outside the harbour full of loose floes come south from the coast of Labrador, and stretching off as far as the eye could see in a solid sheet of unrelieved whiteness, Jonathan discovered another use for the sail loft, connected neither with education nor with sailmaking. He had reached the age of ten that year (a dangerous age for young Newfoundlanders who have developed daring without discretion) and he and Jamie were always into something or other that would have turned their mothers gray with worry had they known about it.

That day the harbour had filled up with small, broken ice pans, mostly ice too small to use as rafts, but big enough for "coppying," an art practised by Newfoundland seal hunters and Newfoundland boys. To coppy over the ice you jump from pan to pan, always leaping to a new pan before the one you are on can sink. In this way you can travel long distances on ice that won't bear your weight if you stand still. You'll get your boots soaking wet, but who cares about that when you can do something so exciting? Sometimes you may even go down to your knees before you can make it to the next pan. At the worst, you'll fall in, but that isn't as bad as it sounds, because you'd have to be some stunned to let yourself sink down out of sight. The water and the ice, between them, will keep you afloat, and then if you can reach a big pan you can drag yourself out. Or of course a friend may help you, if one happens to be handy.

That year a big ship had come into the harbour in winter, and was there now, waiting for the ice to move with an offshore wind. She was anchored in mid stream, well away from the wharves, but near enough to be tempting to experienced ice hands like Jonathan and Jamie.

"Betcha we can coppy out to that there ship and haul ourselves up to the deck on one of them anchor chains," Jamie said.

"Betcha we can," Jonathan agreed, and jumped to the nearest ice pan, just alongside the end of the wharf. Jamie was right behind him. The boys were as nimble as one-year-old dogs, and had no trouble reaching the ship. Sure enough, they found they could grab an anchor chain and hoist themselves up hand over hand, their legs wrapped around the chain and helping to boost them between hand holds.

The chain ran through a hawse pipe, as it usually does in big ships, and came out about a foot and a half below the bow. To hoist yourself to the deck it was necessary to reach up and grab the rail with one hand. As Jonathan did this his mitten slipped (He should have taken it off, of course) he lost his hold, and in a split second he hit the ice and skidded into the water. He went down to his neck.

"Jesus Christ!" Jamie yelled, and went sliding down the anchor chain. It took him several seconds to reach Jonathan and give him a hand up. As he did so, he himself went down to his waist. The boys now found themselves lying prone, half on ice, half in water, wet to the skin.

"Shit!" Jamie said. "Now we've gotta get back ashore right away I s'pose."

"B-b-b-bloody right!" said Jonathan.

As fast as they could, they went coppying back over the ice, not so nimble as they were on the way out, but managing well enough. They climbed up on the wharf stiff with cold and teeth chattering.

"'Twill be warm up in the net loft," Jamie suggested. "Let's get over there quick."

When they arrived at the top of the stairs from the store, squelching salt water at every step, Captain Josh was sitting in the semicircle of sages facing the wood stove and nodding at some point that Magistrate Brennan had just made. He turned his head and cocked a massive eyebrow at his grandson and friend Jamie.

"Well," said he, "will ye jest look at what the cat dragged in — couple o' drowned rats, I'll be bound. Here!" There was a metal spittoon beside the stove, empty — none of those elders would be so low-class as to chew tobacco, but it was there anyway. He pushed it into the middle of the floor. "Take everything off and wring out as much water as ye can manage." He added with a chuckle, to Magistrate Brennan, "That's what we used to do when we were their age, eh?" The boys stripped off their clothes and wrung them into the spittoon, their teeth still chattering. They had to empty the spittoon twice before they were finished. "Now hang everything as handy as ye can get it to the stove pipe," Captain Josh told them. "'Twill soon dry in that heat."

Socks, longjohns, shirts, jackets, jeans and mitts were all hung beside the pot-bellied stove, and soon beginning to send up clouds of steam, while the two miscreants crowded as close as they could get to the heat. Meanwhile one of the men walked over to the wall where outdoor clothes were hung on nails, and came back with two big overcoats, his own and Captain Josh's.

"Here, ye young rapscallions," he said, "get inside o' these, fer the sake o' dacency if fer nothing else."

So they huddled under the coats, which hung over them like tents, and sat on the floor beside the stove.

"If ye can get at least half dry before ye go home, maybe yer mothers won't skin ye alive," someone suggested.

And then the political debate that the boys had interrupted slowly got going again. It seemed to be generally agreed that the Tory Gang in St. John's would never survive next month's budget debate. The underwear and shirts were soon dry enough to wear, though still a little damp. The jeans and jackets took much longer, but finally they too could pass as at least "half dry." By that time the fate of the government had been sealed, and a likely successor for the Prime Minister had been chosen. Then the boys got dressed and went out into the declining daylight of the afternoon, heading up hill where the houses clustered well above the harbour.

"Sure was fun, wasn't it?" Jamie said.

"Sure was!" Jonathan agreed. "Maybe another day we can go after seals if any of 'em come close to land this year. Most likely they'll be beaters, if any of 'em come in at all."

"Beaters is the best of all in a pie," Jamie said, "but some hard to ketch. We'd need a gun."

"I believe I could get a swilin' gun from Uncle Sid," Jonathan said. "He'd loan it to me, I bet, and not let Mother know until afterwards."

"I'd likely get a licking" Jamie said, "'specially if I didn't get a seal."

"Not me," Jonathan said. "Mother gives me a few swats sometimes, but she knows Father and Captain Josh don't hold with it."

"'Twould be worth a lickin' anyway," Jamie said.

"And besides, we *will* get a seal," Jonathan assured him. "Two. One for each of us."

They could almost smell the mouth-watering aroma of flipper pie as they crested the ridge toward their homes.

Creatures of the Wind

Jonathan could see a dozen kites soaring in the sky, each a wooden crucifix dipping with the wind. He had seen pictures of kites in many different patterns flown by men and boys in foreign lands. Some of them looked like dragons or birds or chains of boxes, but here on the coast of Britain's oldest colony just one kind of kite existed: a wooden cross covered with paper, either decorated or plain, and steadied by a long tail of paper bows.

His own kite went into a nosedive behind the rocky knoll, and Jonathan chased after it through the young grass.

A kite, he reflected, was like a ship — it took power from the wind; with a gentle, guiding hand you could make it sail and tack, and live among the clouds. You had to be gentle with a kite, or you'd "sail it under" as he had just done. You must guide it carefully, feeling its response to the wind, allowing for the fact that it had a will of its own.

For a week or so now, it had been kite time. Today was the twenty-fourth of May, the Queen's birthday. The queen in question was long since dead and gone, had been dead since his father was a boy, but her birthday was the cardinal date of spring, now as in former times. This was the day when the most daring of the older boys went swimming for the first time, when men headed off to the gullies up-country with rods and creels and trout flies, and gardeners put their first seeds into the ground. The season for marbles, which started with first mud, when you could scoop the small holes called "mots" out of soft earth, was over. Girls were playing hopscotch and skipping rope. Men were barking nets and steeping sail cloth in great iron cauldrons over open fires, with their bubbling tannin-rich brew inside. Boys were flying kites.

As he ran over the rise, Jonathan saw his grandfather, Captain Joshua, sitting on the rocky outcrop at the very crest of the hill, where he'd have a good view of the harbour and the sea beyond. A rare sight indeed, to see the captain doing nothing. Jonathan loved his grandfather more than anyone, and felt enormously proud of him. The captain was an important man, heavy-set, moustached, benign-looking, commanding great respect when he strolled along the main street of the town, sporting a gold watch chain and a black malacca walking-stick with an ivory handle. The walking-stick served no purpose whatever that Jonathan could see. In another place it might be used to drive off a vicious dog, but there were no vicious dogs in Brigus. It was more like a staff of office, a king's sceptre, identifying its owner as a man of substance, a leader among sailors, almost, if not quite, the equal of the fish merchants themselves.

"I'm his favourite grandchild," Jonathan thought proudly. "Some day maybe I'll be a captain like him."

Far, far back, he was told, there had been another ancestor, Captain Jericho, who, it was said, had organized the fishermen along this shore to take their boats and guns to Carbonear Island, and their families with them, to defend the island against the French in 1697. 'Twas a matter of great pride, he was told, to remember how they had held out against the invaders when all the rest of Newfoundland was sacked and plundered.

Jonathan didn't feel oppressed by the weight of such ancestors. On the contrary, his grandfather and the line of fishing masters and ships' captains that stretched behind him into the remote past gave him confidence. He knew just who he was — latest in a long series of men who had won the world's respect. He could barely remember his great-grandfather, Skipper Cal, but Captain Josh often quoted the old man: "Be not a-feared o' conceit me son. Nary a man is worth a tinker's cuss lest he's conceited." Captain Joshua, who had never gone to school, had books of great weight and importance on his shelf, books like Josephus's *History of the Jews*, and Bishop Usher's sacred chronology. The captain, self-taught with some help from his father, could use chart, compass, and sextant as well as any navigator in the Royal Navy, and he could do what many of them could not: he could figure longitude within a narrow margin by using moon sights.

Jonathan wound in his string and dropped it beside his kite on the grass, then ran up to the captain on the rocks.

"Grandfather!"

"Yes, me son."

"Will you make me a whistle — an alder whistle — if I fetch a gad from the thicket?"

"Ye are old enough to take care o' such foolishness fer yerself," Joshua told him. "Ye are ten, aint ye, going on eleven?"

"Going on twelve, sir. But no one can make a whistle like you can."

"Well ... ye'll have me spoiling ye again, I suppose. "Ye'll have to get over that and learn to rely on yerself when ye go to sea. Here.. He passed Jonathan his clasp knife. "Cut a piece about as thick as yer thumb — a green shoot, and straight, with no twigs, mind."

When Jonathan brought it, the captain trimmed a three-inch piece from the butt-end of the shoot.

"I'd be doin' ye a favour if I used it on yer behind."

Jonathan laughed. His father had told him that Captain Josh had never raised a hand to any child in his life. "Alder's no good for a switch, Captain Josh."

"How long since ye got a licking Johnnie?"

"Got the strap in school last term — just after Christmas."

"Tch-tch! Four months! Teachers do be gettin' some soft nowadays."

Thinking back, Jonathan decided the strap hadn't hurt all that much. The boys who got it often didn't seem to mind it. It was the ones who didn't get it who were intimidated. It wasn't the actual punishment, but the fear of it that kept them in line, mostly the fear that other boys might see them cry.

"Your father never licks you, Johnnie?"

"No sir, never."

"Good. Have me to answer to if 'e did. Wouldn't want any son o' mine beatin' his kids."

"Me'n Father, we get along fine. He's not as good as you, though, at explaining things."

"Doesn't have time fer messin' around with books, like me. That cable office keeps 'im pretty busy."

Joshua rolled the piece of alder back and forth across his knee, tapping the bark with the handle of his knife to loosen it.

"When I was a lad yer age I sailed in an Indiaman, an' the bo'sun used to line up the boys every Monday, an' give us all a taste o' the rope's end — not much, mind — couple o' licks each."

"Why'd he do that?"

"Said the wind'd turn contrary if the boys didn't get a licking once a week. Nonsense, o'course. 'Twas jest an excuse fer keeping us in our place. We were lucky, though — on some ships boys got a real licking every week, not to mention kicks and cuffs in between. Depended on the captain, ye know. Some masters wouldn't allow any youngster to be ill-treated; others didn't care; on their ships boys got no more consideration than dogs ... How'd ye like to sail with me next year, Johnnie? I'll be heading fer Gibraltar, I expect."

"Oh Gee! Can I? Can I really, Captain Josh?"

"Don't say 'O Gee' boy. 'Tis a short form of taking our Lord's name in vain. Yes. Perhaps ye can sail with me next spring. There's fall fish left to be sold every spring these years — merchants waiting fer a higher price. Ye'd miss a couple weeks o' schoolin', but ye are a smart lad, and ye'd catch up aisy enough. 'Course, yer mother mightn't allow it."

"Oh, she will! I'll talk Dad around first, then she'll have a hard time refusing."

"Well, we'll see. It won't be no picnic, mind. We might have one o' those gales that lays ships on their beam ends. Ye never can trust the Western Ocean, winter, spring, or even summer. Ye'd likely be seasick, and scairt half to death."

"I will not!" Jonathan declared indignantly. "Won't be sick. Won't be scairt, either."

The captain looked at him searchingly from under his overhanging eyebrows.

"I believe ye are right, Johnnie. Ye won't be scairt. But ye can't tell beforehand whether ye'll be sick or no. It aint like being out in a trap boat. Even Nelson was seasick. Did ye know that?"

"No sir. I didn't."

Jonathan inherited a strong sense of Brigus history. It was from here that the first skippers had gone to the ice fields. From here the great Captain Bartlett had taken ships further north than any ship had gone before, and then travelled by dog team almost to the North Pole itself, further than any man had gone at that time, making a trail for the explorer Peary to follow. From here one captain after another had gone into the polar ice to rescue stranded American expeditions, reaching them and bringing them back when no one else could do it. "Can I tell Dad you want me to sail with you next spring?"

"Yes, lad. See what 'e says. And maybe I'll take ye again the following winter if all goes well."

"Oh, Captain Josh!" The boy was in his arms, hugging him.

Joshua smiled, and rumpled his hair. "Enough, now! Here. Let me show you how to cut this whistle." He notched it, trimmed a hole in the bark. "Now ye split out that bit of wood, jest abaft the notch. Now replace the bark, careful-like, and blow."

The blast was ear-splitting. Jonathan jumped up and down with delight, blew the whistle again.

"Thank you sir," he shouted, and ran off toward the other boys. "Hey! Look what I've got!"

They were impressed:

"Make one for me, Jonathan."

"Me too."

Kites were reeled in, laid aside, and a great assault on the alder thicket began. Some of the boys had knives, and passed them around. The first whistles weren't too good. Some of them wouldn't sound at all. But they got better with practice, and soon there was a cat-chorus of whistling in various pitches disturbing the air of the high meadow, and competing with the calls of the gulls down along the shore.

But after a while they went back to the kites and retrieved them carefully, to be stored in sheds and porches. The more successful ones might have painted designs added to their sails, or a red bow tied to their tails. Whistles were fun, but kites, creatures of the wind, were part of the true business of childhood. And those who flew kites most skilfully would know, later, how to handle sails — know without being taught.

The End of Summer

The sun poured over the black rocks along shore, infusing them with the heat of late summer, so they were just a shade uncomfortable to Jonathan's feet as he led his two companions over the twists and turns, bumps and hollows of the Cliff Path, but he loved the gentle touch of the smooth lava stone as he threaded his way from ledge to ledge down toward the green clarity of the sea.

To Jonathan the Cliff Path was homeland — one of those places, like the high barrens a mile or so inland, to which he most belonged. It was at his suggestion that his cousin Jimmie, and Jimmie's friend Carlos, both from St. John's, had left their shoes at his house to come exploring the tide pools along this enchanted shore, paddling in water as warm as a caress, water that turned your feet pale green beside the purple starfish and the reddish-brown sea anemones and the false corals that paved the floors of the pools and waited for the return of the tide.

Water in tide pools and water in the sea he thought of as quite different things, but even the sea at this time of year would be tolerable — not warm; not quite icy, either. Thinking about the warmth of late summer made Jonathan reflect that in less than a week he would have to face the trials and troubles of grade eight. His two companions, he supposed, would be going into grade seven in some city school where you had to wear jackets and ties in class, and maybe even line up to march in and out of the room. He resolutely put aside the thought of summer's going; right now the water and the warm rocks, the gem-like greenness of the sea and the living creatures of the shallows were quite enough to think about.

The boys dawdled in the tide pools, picking up starfish and sea urchins, small slippery sponges, and the branching strands of coralline algae that looked like plants from miniature gardens, except that they were not green, but in pastel shades of pink and yellow. Some of the pools were deep, filling hollows of the black lava, so they had to roll their jeans to the knees, and then got the bottoms of them wet anyway. In one of the largest pools, besides slow-crawling periwinkles and limpets and small fragile crabs there was a tiny fish, about an inch and a half long, semi-transparent, but otherwise just like a minnow or a trout. It darted under a clump of weeds that grew out of a crevice, and was gone.

"Once I found a sea horse in a pool like this," Jonathan told his friends.

"Oh. I thought they were big things," Jimmie said. "Did it look like the ones you see in pictures?"

"Yes. It stood upright on its tail in the water, only an inch or two long, and it didn't look the least bit like any other fish. It was reddish-brown, pretty much the same colour as the seaweeds."

They continued downward along the cliff, coming to a broad ledge of rock about six feet above the water, dropping straight into the sea. You could look down through the clear depths, green like the green of a bottle, and see big pebbles covering the bottom, pale gray stones contrasting with the black shelves of rock along shore. A network of sunbeams, reflected from the surge on the surface, danced in slow rhythm over the stones. As he looked down through the water, Jonathan felt joy rising in his heart, the sea was so beautiful.

"It looks about five feet deep," Carlos observed.

"More like eight or ten," Jonathan said. "When the water's as clear as this, it's always deeper than it looks. This is a good place to swim. You can dive here, and it's easy enough to climb out along those rocks over there."

"Isn't it too cold?" Carlos asked.

"Not *too* cold. Let's dive in and find out."

"We don't have any trunks," Jimmie said.

"Don't matter here," Jonathan told him. "It's much nicer swimming in the buff."

They threw off their shirts and jeans and dove rapidly into the sea, straight in line, going deep, touching the smooth rocks of the bottom with their hands, then rising quickly to the surface, spouting water like young whales.

"It *is* cold," Carlos said.

"Stay in a bit and 'twill feel just great," Jonathan told him.

They chased each other in Indian file, diving and rising like porpoises, then climbed over the rocks, one behind the other, and sprawled on the ledge. They were quiet for a minute, enjoying the warm rocks and the warm sun.

"Sure feels great," Carlos observed. He stood up and stretched toward the sky. Jimmie stood too. They locked hands and pushed against each other. Jonathan watched them — suddenly, unexpectedly struck by a powerful sense of the beauty of their bodies.

He had often been naked with other boys, swimming in one of the chain of little lakes just over the hill that stretched northeastward from Brigus, and finally emptied through a river into the sea. Dozens of them went there on summer afternoons, or to the deep pool under the falls in the river. He had a mild sense of self-consciousness about his own body, was inclined to admire himself, to strut about a bit, showing off, whether there was anyone to see him or not. This, somehow, was quite different. For the first time it wasn't his own body that interested him, but those of the other boys. They were, he realized, beautiful. He had always associated beauty with landscape or with the cloudy moods of the sky or the savage moods of the sea, with gardens, with the colours of sunset. Here, for the first time, he understood the beauty of nude humans. This was what the artists were saying when they painted angels or gods or girls bathing. There were hundreds of such pictures in the art books at the library, jealously guarded by the librarian, for fear of vandalism and defacement. The artists had been looking at people the way he now looked at those companions of his: Jimmie, a sturdy, squarely-built youngster with dark-toned skin, like a boy from Spain or Italy, with curly hair now shedding water, his sides gleaming in the sun, his young penis hanging neat between his legs, his stubby toes square and firm on the rocks. Jimmie looked like someone you'd want to hug, like a teddy bear. But it was Carlos he found most attractive. The strange boy stood naked and slender, smiling slightly at him, his body like a pale flame against the black rocks, pale hair shining like a flag, pale feet slender and beautiful, his firm penis like the cone of a young fir, standing out above his rounded testicles.

To Jonathan the strange boy looked tender and vulnerable, but filled for all that with life and spirit. He wanted to stand up, to reach out and touch Carlos, to touch those sculptured shoulders, run his fingers down that tender body, take the boy's hands, perhaps, touch his hips and thighs.

He did none of those things. Instead, he lay back against the rock in the sun with half-closed eyes, while they began the sort of teasing horse-play that boys everywhere seem to enjoy. Jimmie made a playful grab for his friend's penis. The other boy dodged away, and tripped him, so that he somersaulted into the water. Carlos dived after him, and Jonathan watched the two bodies, pale green beneath the surface, cutting the water like arrows, trailing bubbles, miraculous in their beauty. Then Jimmie and Carlos climbed the rocks once more, and began wrestling playfully, not really struggling, but play-fighting with each other. Jonathan watched, wanting to join their game, but decided there was no way three boys could wrestle together at the same time.

"Hey, Jimmie," he said. "We could wrestle while we dry in the sun, but there's no room on the ledge. Why don't we climb up to the meadow?"

"Sure," Jimmie said. "Lots of room on the grass. Let's do that." It was only a few yards to the little meadow — an abandoned potato field that sloped down almost to the edge of the cliff above the sea. They were there in seconds.

"You guys wrestle first," Jonathan suggested, "and whichever one can pin the other one can wrestle me next."

"And whichever one comes last gets held down and tickled till he hollers 'enough,'" Jimmie suggested.

"Nothing like that," Jonathan said, "but the loser can wrestle me afterwards." That way, he reflected, he'd get to play with both of them.

Jonathan watched them wrestle, this time really struggling together, Jimmie getting the better of it ... What about girls, he wondered? Why didn't girls swim with boys and play in the sun afterwards? Except for really little kids he had never seen a girl in the nude. Would a girl be as beautiful as Carlos? Perhaps not. She'd be plumper perhaps, thicker in the legs, without that willowy slenderness. Still ... different. He tapped Jimmie on the shoulder.

"That's enough," he said. "You've had him pinned at least three seconds."

Carlos lay full length on his back in the sun, and Jonathan tickled his ribs with his toes. "Better rest up," he said. "You can take me on after I've given Jimmie his trouncing."

It didn't take long, in fact. Though they were almost the same weight, Jonathan was stronger than his young cousin, and fresher. Jimmie squirmed and twisted, but soon lay still, with his shoulders on the grass.

"Hey, Carlos," Jonathan said, "how about bringing a straw to tickle his nose?"

"No!" Jimmie shouted. He'd had straws put into his nose before, driving him half out of his mind. "Not fair, Jonathan!"

"I was only kidding," Jonathan told him, letting him go, cuffing him gently. "OK, your turn," he told the other boy.

Wrestling with Carlos, Jonathan didn't try too hard, wanting to make the game last, working just enough to keep the younger boy struggling hard. Carlos wrestled vigorously for a while, then subsided tired out, lying quiet with Jonathan's arms around him, Jonathan feeling a powerful surge of tenderness for this young stranger.

"I wish you could stay," he said impulsively. "I sure wish you could stay, instead of going back to St. John's." But just then Jimmie gave him a gentle kick.

"Hey," he said, "you guys going to lie there all day?"

"Yes, we should dress and go home," Jonathan agreed, sitting up. "It's getting on for supper time."

They retrieved their clothes from the rocks, reluctantly pulled them on, and walked up through the meadow to the road. Just three days, Jonathan reflected, and Jimmie and Carlos would be back in the city. He'd miss them, especially Carlos, the magic boy he had discovered just this afternoon, just a bit too late.

But he knew, too, that something irreversible had happened, something deep within himself. Life would never be quite the same again.

Autumn Meeting

It is the time of year — and the time of life — for solitary walks. Jonathan is back in school, but his heart is on the hills and in the sky. School counts for very little compared with the countryside, the pervasive sense of sweet melancholy that he finds there, and the brooding sense of eternity that seems to transpire from this land where his people have lived and died for uncounted generations. Weekends, when school is closed — that is the time when life has its chance to happen at deep levels, to move in new directions, even when little on the surface seems to have changed.

On a crystal-clear morning of Indian summer he is abroad soon after daybreak; his feet are chilled with dew, and dripping shrubs have wet him to the knees, but there is promise of warmth to come: sunshine lies like frost on the meadow making myriad little rainbows of the dewdrops, each small fire blending through red, yellow, green, to deepest indigo and violet.

The beaver pond lies deep and dark in the shadow of the hill. Around its bank and over the dam, beneath willows and birches, runs a narrow path, its clay patted smooth by the feet of ten generations. Thousands of boys through three centuries have circled its banks in the hot afternoons of hundreds of summers, plunging down to its green depths (Last one in's a horse's ass) shouting, calling to one another, throwing one another into the water, creating transient brotherhoods that continuously dissolve but forever gain new recruits from new generations of brothers, cousins, the occasional stranger. Jonathan knows that his father and his uncles frequented this tiny lake years before he was born — and before that his grandfather, and other ancestors who were the boys of an earlier age. But even before they ceased being boys they were gone — into fishing boats, onto the decks of schooners, the younger ones replacing them, welling up from below like a spring. There is a sense of timelessness here.

As he rounds the bend toward the dam he sees the girl Virginia, a girl from his grade eight class, a girl who has walked home from school with him once or twice — they live along the same road. But today she does not look like a schoolgirl in skirt and ankle socks and blouse; she looks like a boy — like Jonathan, she has blue jeans that are soaked to the knees, and bare feet, her toes gleaming wet, the colour of old ivory, like piano keys in his grandmother's dim parlour.

"Hi, Jonathan."

"Hi, Virginia. Going somewhere?"

"Just walking. Getting myself soaked, like you."

They fool around the edge of the pond for a minute or two.

"The frogs are all gone," she observes, "down in the mud, I suppose, waiting for spring ... Want to climb the hill into the sunshine?"

"Sure."

Together they climb the ridge above the valley, find a mossy patch, and lie there, warming themselves in the early morning sun and watching the clouds sail like clipper ships across the sky. The stream that runs beside them down to the beaver pond laughs lightly as it falls over the stones. She moves close to him. Shyly, she reaches for his hand. Then her feet find his, touching gently.

Their garments will be better hung on the shrubs to dry. Jonathan cannot remember, afterwards, who suggests this, for they seem to know each other's thoughts. The girl is like a mirror-image of himself, he thinks — even her hair the colour of his own, a kind of dark reddish copper — but no, not a mirror-image, more like an image in water, vaguely like himself, but different, as though they were on the sea bottom with net-like lines of light waving over hands and faces.

"Do you think it's too cold to swim?" she asks.

Jonathan is almost speechless. "I ... I've never ... with a girl ..."

"Let's pretend we're both boys," she says. She is smiling, impishly. "Nobody comes here, this time of year."

He stands, lifting her gently to her feet, and they reach, without preamble, for buttons and zippers, shucking the kernel from the husk, the nut from the shell, each revealing the other — shirts first, exposing the sculptured beauty of bare shoulders, the swell of firm breasts, the curving downsweep to waist and hips — and then the slide of zipper and the slow stripping downward of blue denim until each stands naked and perfect, astonished, almost overpowered by the beauty of the other.

Then they step away together toward the water, toward the fringe of cattails and the bending willows. She is lean like a young willow, he thinks, but gilded by the early sun. He puts an arm about her waist, and guides her into the pond.

The water is chill from the night, from the days of autumn that have passed over it before this brief return of summer, and it is black under the shadows of the trees where the sky does not reflect. It closes about them in a cold caress. They wade and splash each other, then duck in and swim strongly, but only for a few moments. Then they rise together, their cold bodies touching, nipple touching nipple, lip brushing lip, moving with a gentleness, a tenderness, a sacramental union that has nothing in it of agony, no urge toward sexual completion, but a wonderful sense of its own completeness, a whole that is both two and one, fulfilled in a way that one alone can never be. They walk hand in hand through the willows, and up to the sun-warmed hill, the tall, soft heads of timothy whipping them gently as they pass.

"Maybe," Jonathan suggests, as they retrieve their clothes and struggle into them, the job made difficult by the wetness of their bodies, "we could go to town together this afternoon — to a movie or something?"

"Yes. Let's go. I'd like that."

Again they can read each other's thoughts: People will see them together, connect them, know that they have formed a partnership. They feel proud of this, proud of each other.

"Maybe we could do our homework together, too," she suggests.

"Sure. Get it all done, for a change." Even his mother would approve of this. He laughs. "We can work at my house. I'm sure Mother will give us cookies and mugs of cocoa, to keep us going."

"I've never been very close with my mother," she confides — "not exactly cuddling up to her, you know. How about yours?"

"No problems," Jonathan assures her.

"Well ... mine's more like a teacher ... When I first began to menstruate ..." She pauses. "You know about menstruation?"

"Yes. It's what happens once a month, with girls. You bleed a bit, don't you? And there's some pain?"

"Not always pain. But there's always blood, yes. Well, Mother never told me a thing about it, never warned me what would happen. And when it started one day, I thought I was bleeding to death. Bleeding *down there* you know was really awful, like something had broken inside."

"What did you do?"

"I tried to stop it, with tissues, and a pad, and it seemed to dry up, and then later it started again, and I panicked, and finally told Mother I was bleeding. And do you know what she said? She said, 'Oh, that's nothing. That's just The Curse.'"

"The curse?" Jonathan is puzzled.

"It's in the Bible, Mother says."

"And is it?"

"I don't know. Something about Adam and Eve and the apple, I think."

"Is that all your mother said?"

"That's all. I asked the nurse about it later on, and that's when I really found out that it isn't even bleeding in the usual sense. I mean, it's not something getting damaged or anything like that. It's just some tissue getting shed, each month, stuff that would grow into a baby if you'd been with a man at the right time. It goes on every month until you're pregnant, or until you're too old to have kids. Then it stops."

"Is it tough luck, being a girl?" Jonathan asks.

"No. I don't think so. Boys have their problems too, don't they?"

"I'm glad you're a girl, anyway."

They pause by Jonathan's gate. Virginia will have to walk onwards another quarter mile to reach her house. He'd like to kiss her, but it is much too public a place for that — and much too soon anyway, unless you are both naked in a swimming pond. In spite of what has passed between them, Jonathan feels a little shy with her. He'll have to overcome it, he realises, have to begin — what did they call it? — *wooing* her. What a stupid word, he thinks. He touches her hand, and their fingers lock for a moment.

"I'll come by your house right after lunch," he promises.

"See you then."

He watches her walk away, her body moving like a song, and he whispers to himself, "I love you." It will be a long while before he can say it out loud.

Love and Frustration

When Jonathan first met Sarah he had already started his post-graduate year at Toronto. It didn't happen at a party, or in a lecture room. Instead, she flitted lightly across his peripheral vision, not once, but time and again, until he focused more deliberately on the elusive figure, and eventually spoke to her one day as they entered a library building together.

Both, as it happened, were unattached and fancy-free. Their eyes locked in an unspoken flash of understanding — he seemed to be looking deep into layers of crystal light shot through with colour. They smiled, reading each other's thoughts, and in mere minutes Jonathan knew that this was not one of those casual attractions that were so common and so ephemeral; this was the real thing, the first great love of his life since he and Virginia had parted so long, long ago. There was none of the sparring and flirting that had marked the affairs of his past six or seven years. Almost without words, their souls spoke across the void that isolates people on their private islands, one from the other.

Sarah, he noted, was beautiful, but the idea seemed almost banal compared to what he felt; he'd met many beautiful women before, and had never reacted to them this way. She had a light playfulness about her, but he had played with many people of both sexes without feeling committed from the depths of his being, as he felt now. Love is a mystery — a mystery doubly compounded when it is returned, as it was in this instance, from their first moment together. Something was happening to the two of them, something vastly important, and beyond their understanding, something close to life's core and purpose.

"God! Why haven't we met before?"

"I don't know. I was thinking exactly the same thing."

Those were almost the first words that passed between them, but words had nothing to do with it. No wonder that people in classical times believed such matters were written in the stars!

"Do you suppose we've been speaking to each other unconsciously, with body language?" she asked.

"Probably," he said, "though I was hardly aware of your existence until now. I'd rather believe that you were my queen and my sister in an Egyptian incarnation four thousand years ago."

She laughed. "Such nonsense!"

"Yes, of course. But don't you agree that we need myths to help keep our lives glued together?"

She seemed to consider this for a moment, then shook her head. "Let's not talk about myths. Let's get through whatever is the most pressing work we have to do today — preferably in the next fifteen minutes. And then ... It's still summer outside, and there are about ten miles of parkland stretching up the Humber Valley into North York."

"Ah yes," he said, "a picnic! And maybe a swim in the pellucid waters of the Humber."

"Jonathan! You want to catch the mange?"

"Well ... didn't I hear somewhere that they'd chlorinated the Humber? Or we could take along our own jug of chlorine."

"Speaking of jugs ... I'd rather follow the Fitzgerald recension of the *Rubaiyat*. You know:

A book of verses underneath the bough,
A jug of wine, a loaf of bread — and thou....

I'm not sure about the singing part. I don't sing. Do you?"

"Is it too soon to say I love you?" he asked.

She laughed, and hugged him, right there among the stacks of sociology tomes.

And that's how it began.

It did, of course, progress and deepen. They did not know by intuition that they were both enamoured of the same English poets, that they listened to the same kinds of music, from early baroque to late romantic, that they both loved forests and rivers and mountains — or that they both felt the same lonely isolation in the midst of a society that was so crude, so cruel, so viciously selfish. There's an old belief that opposites attract each other. Maybe that's true for a one-night stand. For a prolonged relationship common interests are essential. It took months, even years, for all this to come together, but come together it did.

That first evening, under the trees beside the Humber, she took his hand and laced her fingers through his. She kissed him lightly. Such kisses, fleeting pledges of total commitment, were as close an intimacy as they enjoyed that first day. Love may begin like a lightning stroke, but its development should not be rushed. They both seemed to know and to agree on this.

Just the same, they would soon have to contrive, somehow, to live together off campus; the place for lovers is in each other's arms, not in separate beds. By the end of the Christmas recess that proved to be easy enough. They returned with small sums of grant money and a small legacy from Sarah's father (who hadn't lived with Sarah's mother since Sarah was a child). By stretching matters they were able to rent a half-bare small apartment for the remainder of the semester. They moved their few possessions into the tight downtown space, and began camping there. (They didn't think of it as *living* in the regular sense.)

There was a table and a gas stove and a cupboard in the little kitchenette, but they had none of the implements of housekeeping none of those essential gadgets for toasting and mixing and cooking, only a primitive coffee pot, and some salvaged plastic dishes designed for public picnics. Sarah insisted on one purchase at least: real wine glasses. And they drank real wine — not vintage, exactly, but dry table wine that you could drink without gagging. That was the nearest they came to even a touch of respectability. They had no such thing as a table cloth, no cocktail shaker, no vacuum cleaner, not even a bedspread. The place was full of books, mostly borrowed from the libraries.

Sarah, who owned neither nightgown nor pyjamas, had one sumptuously luxurious garment — a silk robe of imperial purple — the famous red-purple of the Romans — with brocade for ornament and a sash for a fastener. It was typical of her that she would own this elegant robe, and lack a second pair of shoes. Between laughs, she quoted something attributed to Wilde: "So long as I have the luxuries, I can do without the necessities."

Jonathan loved her in her habitual *dishabille*, barefoot, naked under silk, the half-open robe revealing the sweeping curves of her supple body and the tight contours of her lovely breasts, pale and blue-veined.

"That rich purple against your ivory skin almost drives me crazy," he told her.

She laughed. "Don't you dare attack me. I'm not a sex object."

"It's not lust exactly," he told her; "something between lust and aesthetic pleasure. Where does the one end and the other begin? I could just sit here and watch you forever."

"I'd get tired of that," she told him.

"I suppose it was pleasure like this that the popes enjoyed while viewing Michelangelo's paintings."

"I'm no expert on Michelangelo," she said, "but I have an idea he was less interested in beautiful young women than in muscular young men. His Sistine Chapel paintings look to me like delights for the eyes of homo-erotic ascetics. Didn't a puritan pope order G-strings painted on some of his naked figures?"

"Yes. Why some figures and not others? Did the pope pick out the ones that gave him an erection? In any case, a later pope ordered those defacements removed."

"It all seems curiously childish nowadays, doesn't it?"

"Yes, it does, but there's no doubt such high art can be sexually stimulating, and that's what got old Michie his commissions. After a visit to the Sistine Chapel the cardinals would dash off for a visit with an experienced altar boy or a willing acolyte."

"Jonathan, you have an evil mind. What's wrong with sexual stimulation?"

"Nothing. It's much better than the Colosseum or the jousting ring, that's for sure. A society that accepts a generous amount of joyful eroticism is likely to be peaceful, as

Byzantium was. But then, of course, the barbarians start pounding on the gates."

"Anyway, I like the erotic art of the Italian Renaissance," Sarah said. "Not Michelangelo particularly, but those nearly naked teenage angels (Are they boys or girls? Nymphets, anyway) in the great church paintings of the sixteenth century. Whatever they are, boy, girl, or hermaphrodite, I wouldn't mind having one for a pet."

"I thought women weren't supposed to be addicted to the lust of the eye," Jonathan said.

"You said yourself it isn't lust, exactly," she reminded him. "And anyway, there isn't nearly so much difference between the sexes as your patriarchal society liked to pretend. It isn't 'beefcake' that turns us on, either. We can be as delighted by a beautiful teenage angel, boy or girl, as any cardinal."

"Sarah ... seriously ... I think you're the equal of any angel in a Mazzola painting."

"Well ... thank you, kind sir. But ... Mazola ... isn't that pure corn?"

Jonathan refused to be distracted. "You're a little riper, fortunately."

"Than the corn, you mean? ... Hey! don't throw that book! I think I know what you mean. I'm more touched with mortality, perhaps."

"I'll love you forever," he said.

"A long road, that," she said soberly.

He sat there, thoughtful. Forever, if it lasted full term, might include eyes that had faded, skin that had wrinkled and sagged, faces that perhaps had taken on lines from life's bitterness. Unendurable thought — and yet ... yes, there might be aspects of their union that could transcend even age and the withering of all that physical beauty. Could that be? He wasn't sure. He merely hoped that it might be so, and that they might in some distant time become those rarest of human creatures, not only lifelong lovers, but people who were still beautiful in old age.

"To me, you know, you are still something of a stranger," he said. "That may be part of your great attraction."

"We're not quickly or easily intimate — either of us," she said.

Thinking back, Jonathan felt that he had been more intimate with his first love, Virginia, than with anyone later on. At least they seemed to have been totally frank with each other — there was really nothing they would not discuss — but that had lasted through an autumn, a winter, and a spring. Then there were only temporary relationships in highschool and college.

Sarah was completely different from Virginia. She had none of that quick eagerness to communicate, no wish to express her feelings in gush or hyperbole. There was a pool of reserve at her centre, like the reserve that Jonathan found in himself. They were vocal mainly on an intellectual level. Others, it seemed, might be vocal mainly on the emotional level. There were many things that they never discussed at all. When they played at experimental sex, at the novelties of the *Kama Sutra*, fetishism and sex fantasies, they never discussed them. There would always be such elements in their relationship, presumably, but they remained unspoken. Jonathan supposed that this might be a residue from the puritanism that had pervaded North America for centuries. In his early teens he had almost broken out of it, but complete escape from deeply imprinted culture is very difficult, and you are more than likely, in the fullness of time, to find yourself repeating the errors of your parents.

How do you know which of their attitudes were errors? Perhaps a certain reserve between lovers is desirable. Is total immersion in each other's thoughts and desires actually the best relationship for a man and a woman? Didn't those couples who acted out their fantasies in the bedroom with leather and fur and black lace and whatnot all end in the divorce courts within a few months or years?

"I'm not sure about that," Sarah told him. "Perhaps most couples tend to become incompatible after a while, whether they live down each other's throats or not. They suffer disappointment, estrangement. Then, some readjust, and some don't. Among the strongest unions I know are those between people who separated for a while, then came together again."

"With us there'll be no separation."

"No. I'm convinced there won't be. Indeed, I'm absolutely certain of it."

They were lucky in their careers — at least so far as having them match geographically. After their post-graduate year they got jobs teaching at high schools in Halifax — a city that struck them both as very uptight after the free-swinging atmosphere that Jonathan had gotten used to in St. John's and Sarah in Toronto. There was a great deal of "Keep off the grass" and "Ties must be worn" and "Park only in designated areas" and so on. There were street kids of both sexes offering their bodies for sale — in designated areas — but the pretense of respectability was universal, and stifling. The glitz and false fronts were everywhere.

"And what about those students we spend so much time with?" Sarah asked. "Aren't they disappointing? Don't you find them almost Victorian in their attitudes?"

"Yes. They become what they've been taught, and as kids they were taught to be puritans — even prudes. Many of the boys won't take showers together. They feel the need to hide away in a booth before changing into a pair of gym shorts."

"Well, I suppose they'll get over it, later."

"Sure. Their parents go tom-catting around, goodness knows, but they don't do it with a clear conscience. No matter how many spouses and so-called lovers they run through, they always feel they're committing adultery."

"Perhaps that's an essential part of the fun."

Jonathan thought of Eve in the Garden of Eden: "Ye shall not eat of it, neither shall ye touch." Woe to those who have been taught to mistrust the touch of fellow humans. Consciously or otherwise, the puritan regarded touching as the first step into sin — or perhaps the second step. The first step might be a smile. If he smiled warmly at one of his students while explaining a figure of speech he might see her face become defensive. He felt sorry for such emotionally crippled children on the way to becoming emotionally frigid adults. They'd learn to *fuck* of course. Practically everyone did, empty as the activity might prove to be. But they might never learn to love.

"And it isn't our job to teach them, much as we might wish it were," he said. "According to the education system's unwritten code, our job is to teach them certain skills, and perhaps a bit of propaganda in favour of so-called democracy, certainly not to help them become human."

"Teachers who try it may be heading for trouble with parents, boards, or the principal," Sarah pointed out.

"Child abuse," Jonathan said. "Those children have been truly abused, just as truly as if they'd been mauled by the archetypal wicked uncle, and, I suppose, many of them will pass the abuse along to their own children, if they ever have any."

"Have you read Samuel Butler's novel *The Way of All Flesh*?" Sarah asked.

"No. I must admit I haven't. It isn't much read, nowadays."

"It's about abuse, and how it is passed along from generation to generation. And it was written back around 1880. Butler sure didn't fit into the society of his time, and fifty years later, we certainly don't fit into this society."

Jonathan looked more morose than usual. "The trouble is, *nobody* fits into it. It just isn't made for humans — what do you suppose it is made for — the corporations?"

"Well ..." Sarah laughed, "they do seem to be truly at home here, don't they? and I suppose if we were doing our duty by those youngsters we'd be trying to help them fit into the corporate structures, instead of trying to open magic casements for them, and so on."

"We'd have to be teaching economics or sociology, wouldn't we?"

"Of course. Economics. Political science. Sociology. Law. Tax Evasion. So where does poor old Keats fit in? Nowhere, obviously — nowhere at all."

So highschool teaching was mostly disappointment and frustration, as so many teachers had found out before them. But it didn't go on forever. A few years later they'd be back in central Canada teaching at a university. And that, of course, would be a wholly different scene.

Meanwhile, if work wasn't all that gratifying, their private lives blossomed together, and their vacations, usually spent in Newfoundland, were not always sunny, but always included vistas of breathtaking delight, not invariably through magic casements, but often including the foam of perilous seas.

"This really is a world apart," Sarah said during her first visit. "I'm amazed that you were able to leave it."

"I haven't left it," Jonathan said. "Like the old sea dogs who were my ancestors, I'm merely earning a living as a travelling man. Some day, when we can afford it, we'll come back here to live."

"Is that a promise?"

"Not really a promise, Sarah. It's a vow."

A Summer Place

They sat on a low rise above the harbour with its small wooded island the only wild patch of ground inside the town. They came here every summer recuperating from the toil of teaching highschool in Halifax, and whenever the weather was fine they were outdoors.

Below them a church was outlined against the sea. It looked to be far below, because the scale of everything in Brigus was deceptive. Above the church the dark water of the harbour spread out on either hand. Then the hills. But there, above the hills was a bank of cloud hanging over the open sea with a glimpse of ocean above it, and above that again the distant blue line of land running out to Cape St. Francis, with the sky over that — a seven-layered landscape of change and contrast.

In winter those hills would be grimly groined in gray and white — no ski slopes there! just the rock of the earth's crust into which plants have made no visible penetration as yet. Houses, a wharf, a few trees clung to the water's edge, but above this scant promise of civilisation the land rose as uncompromising as the mountains of the moon.

"You'd wonder why people ever chose to live in such a place, in spite of its beauty," Sarah remarked.

"Perhaps the first ones were sort of stranded here, at the end of a fishing voyage," Jonathan suggested, "and then, perhaps, they discovered that they had learned to love it. You know, it wasn't until I returned here from college that I realized how small this place is — not just its size, but the compactness — the way it fits down into this little hollow between the hills. And how rugged everything is!"

"It certainly is picturesque."

"More than that. Tortured landscape. If you climb that naked hill between here and Cupids you'll see rocks that look like giant plough ridges stretching away for miles and miles in perfect parallels — the strata turned until they're perpendicular — and fields of black and gray and green lichens announcing the passing of the ice age. We took it all for granted when we were kids. That little valley where the highway comes down from the Barrens, with the few fields on either side, is about the only way in or out of here, except for a rock climber."

"It was the harbour that mattered, I suppose, to the ... ah ... Did you call them pioneers?"

"Settlers."

"Yes. Roving fishermen who settled here, of course."

"And they made a life out of it — a good life, after a few generations. This was a civilised town, with a transplanted culture. Did you know that all the trees in Brigus were brought here from England? That graveyard near the harbour is still overgrown with Scotch broom and English rowan, and the kind of hawthorn that English people call 'the May.'"

"It's easy to visualize the past here," she said. "You can almost *feel* it."

"The further back you go the dimmer it becomes, of course," Jonathan replied. "It's no trouble for me to see back past my father who stayed ashore and worked in an office, or my mother, who was a very conventional woman of her time, but beyond my grandfather.."

"What about your grandmother? There was just one, wasn't there?" Sarah asked.

"At home, yes. A warm, nurturing women. She made up for my mother's sternness, the lickings I got when I was little. And then, of course, there was Captain Josh. It's pretty hard to see past *him*, alright. He's a sort of roadblock barring the way to his own ancestors. But I remember a bit about my great-grandmother."

"That would be the captain's mother?"

"Yes — a tall, monumental woman, like a figure carved from gray granite, facing the sea alone because her husband was so often away, winter and summer. She had a lot to do with making Captain Josh the man he was, I'm sure."

"And making you into a kind of image of him," she suggested.

"Oh, is that the way you see me? I'm flattered."

"You don't remember much of your great-grandfather?"

"Captain Cal. I remember a little. He was a seaman, too, of course, and his father before him — and so on. It's easier to imagine the history of the men, but the women had even more to do with making the life here, because they stayed at home, while the men roved abroad. So far as I remember anything about my great-grandmother, her main quality was endurance. A lot of the settlers must have been like that — making lives for themselves and their children in a semi-barren land surrounded by ice floes and seal herds, with the occasional white bear visiting from the Arctic, and the endless piles of gleaming fish fetched out of the cold sea."

"It must have been a very harsh life — almost like primitive hunters," Sarah mused.

"Well — there was warmth back there too — human warmth, and the comfort they built around them, the physical protection: houses so solid they could take whatever the sky decided to send down, huge open hearths with logs blazing under iron pots, beds piled deep with layer upon layer of goose down sealed in cloth."

"You make it sound like an elaborate cocoon. What about the human warmth?"

"Children, of course, chilled by snow squall or spindrift, could climb into the arms of the nearest adult — anyone. If you were a child, your world was full of surrogate parents. There were no such things as strangers, not to mention dangerous ones. The huge hairy dog would lie in his place at the chimney corner, enjoying the luxury of sharing human life, being part of that strongly-built family, the cat between his paws, dreaming of mice."

"That's where you're using your imagination," Sarah laughed. "How do you know the cat was dreaming of mice?"

"Because cats always do. Haven't you watched them, paws twitching, jaws ready to snap?"

"Now with me," Sarah said, "it's completely different. I can hardly get further back than my mother. There was a great aunt. I have a few of her things — trifles, really: a little clock in an alabaster case, a jewel box in veined onyx — not collector's stuff, but things you couldn't buy today, though it may have been dime store trade fifty years ago.

We visited grandparents occasionally, at Christmas or Thanksgiving, but I never really knew any of them, and now I only see my mother once or twice a year. I suppose I could ask her about her parents, but it hardly seems worth while — it's like I belong just to myself, almost without ancestors."

"Spoken like a true North American!" Jonathan exclaimed. "How long do you suppose this current social structure will last?"

"I've no idea, have you?"

"It's falling apart already. Another generation, and we'll have something completely different. Meanwhile I like to keep alive the connection to the past, all the way back to that early ancestor who made the first voyage to the seal hunt, Captain Malachi."

"Tell me about it, and about the women who stayed home, raising the children, wondering if the men would ever come back."

"Well, Captain Malachi, once he started going for seals in half-decked shallops, soon graduated to a small schooner with a crew of ten or eleven relatives. Three of them could handle the little ship easily enough, but you always took as many hands as you could stow on board for sealing. A dozen men could fill the small ship with three or four thousand pelts, if they got right into the fat.

"His wife Sephina worked as hard as any of them at the fitting out, made sealskin boots for all hands, stitched on soles of cowhide, made sure they all had underwear of real wool flannel that would keep a man alive even if he was caught out in a blizzard over night.

"And then they went off. They'd be gone six weeks, eight weeks and every night of those weeks she'd be on her knees, beside the cod oil lamp, praying for their safety. Some of those men were her sons and nephews, perhaps a brother. But she did more than pray. She did a man's work while they were gone, keeping the fires, knitting nets for the spring fishing, feeding and teaching the children — there were no schools then, of course."

"You've heard all this from your family."

"Yes. I'm not making it up. But there was nothing special about it. That's how it was with colonial women. And every night after the first four weeks she'd be up on the lookout, peering into the seaward gloom, searching for a light, for the yellow gleam of an oil lamp at a masthead. And finally, after thirty nights, or forty, or fifty, she'd see it. It happened every year. Until one year when she was already an old woman, no longer in charge of things, having yielded leadership to her sons and their wives, the nights went on and on, fifty, sixty, seventy, hope gradually fading, because, of course, their luck had finally run out, and no trace of Captain Malachi and his crew of relatives was ever found."

"What about widows? How did they manage?"

"Well, if they didn't have grown sons, or brothers, or other close relatives, the more distant ones looked after them — cousins, neighbours ... they were never left destitute, or thrown on public charity. If they were young enough, they often remarried. A few widowed women took guns and went hunting; others went fishing, not for trade, but to provide food for winter. It wasn't considered proper for women to do this, but they did it anyway, when they had to."

"It all seems so long ago," Sarah said, "like a different world."

"That's what it was," Jonathan agreed, "but it was a world that lasted down to my own childhood. Let me describe a few things I remember. There was a public grindstone, where everybody sharpened their axes, some boy turning the stone while a man held the blade against the wet rock. There was a mill, further in the bay, with a huge water wheel for sawing logs into lumber. Every woman in Brigus baked her own bread, and some of them used hops instead of yeast for leavening. Neighbours sometimes offered me glasses of goat's milk. It tasted strange to me, but I liked it. I once had sealskin boots, made by a local cobbler from skins tanned in St. John's. I had a great uncle who operated a smoke house for curing salmon and herring. It was a great gift to take to your relatives in the city — packets of kippers or slabs of smoked salmon. In the middle of our main road, at an intersection, there was a huge tree left standing, the road passing both sides of it. They said it was planted by the first settlers, three centuries ago. When I was a very small child my father took me to Harbour Grace to see the airplanes getting ready for the first transatlantic flights. The chance of reaching Europe alive in one of those planes was slim. Some of them crashed just trying to get off the ground."

"It's frightening to think how the world is changing," Sarah said. "Do you think we're ready for it?"

"Of course not," Jonathan said. "Whenever change on such a scale might happen, you could never be ready for it. Perhaps that's why the world in our time seems to be such an unmitigated disaster."

"And now it seems people here are no longer fishing, hunting seals, but merely catering to visitors," she said.

"Actually it's a long time since any sealing was done out of Brigus. There was a great fleet of wooden sealing ships here in the days of my great-great grandfather, but that only lasted about eighty years. The last load of seal sculpts was landed here in 1884. The two small factories that we had here, curing pelts and rendering fat into oil for export, closed down. After that, the men who went seal hunting had to sail out of St. John's. And there was no more fishing from here after 1935. But of course there was still a big inshore fishery out of Cupids, right next door, and we still had sailors and ships' captains, but they sailed out of other ports."

"So Brigus now is a sort of retirement centre," she said.

"Yes, and all the young ones leaving home," he added. "You know, leaving home seems to be almost a law of human nature to us in North America. We tend to think it's universal, like birds leaving the nest — so many boys and girls feel they're in a trap, that above all they must get out of the dead little town on the prairie, or the hideous rural slum on Cape Breton Island. We're tempted to think it happens everywhere and always, but it was nothing like that in Europe before the Industrial Revolution, or in Newfoundland when I was a child. Even then, you might be forced to leave home because making a living in a fishing outport was so difficult. Women sometimes left Conception Bay and went off to work in Boston. But, if you left, it was much against your will, and even if you never came back, the beautiful little harbours would be forever in your mind, the gulls keening overhead, the salmon leaping in the sun, the sunkers sounding beside the headlands."

They sat quietly as the evening came on, and the warm twilight descended. Then a westering moon appeared above the hills, a crescent casting its light down through the valley, over the roofs of Brigus to the sea.

The town was silent now, soft lights beginning to glimmer from the windows of fine old houses that had once served as shore bases for world-ranging captains, now purchased and "renovated" as summer places for millionaire business people from St. John's. So Jonathan and Sarah walked quietly hand in hand down the main road of the village to their own summer place, an old house that took in paying guests, within sight and sound of the last smithy, where fires continued to roar, and an old smith, nearing ninety, continued to forge decorative iron work for summer places, just as he had once forged ship's hardware for the last schooners in the coastal trade when Jonathan was a child.

Paddling through Academia

Kirk Fitzgibbon Ph.D. leaned over the coffee machine waiting for the last drips to drop.

"It's sabbatical for you next year I hear," Jonathan said. "Wonder will I ever make it to a sabbatical?"

"No reason why not," Kirk said. "This'll be my third — same job for twenty years."

"And made Vice-Chair," Jonathan added. "The reward of brilliance, research, and dedicated committee work."

"Thank you." Kirk grinned. "I do it to get ahead. My real interests are elsewhere, as I guess you know."

"Yes, Kirk, everyone knows you're a mystic — not in a class with Nicholas of Cusa or Plotinus, perhaps, but into reincarnation, bodily auras..."

"And secret wisdom handed down from the builders of the pyramids, don't forget that part."

"All of it contrary to science and common sense," Jonathan said.

"Right. I'm not a scientist. Like you, I'm a humanist. As for common sense, I prefer the uncommon kind. I get to do some of the elementary things all the time, and things a bit more far out during my sabbaticals."

"It was Polynesia last time, wasn't it?"

"Yes. And Australasia. Come over to my office and I'll show you a couple photos."

"Now this is just a fishing picture, me and my prize catch. Only thing a bit unusual about it is the kind of fish — you might call it a man-eating shark, a tiger. Caught it inside the Great Barrier Reef. Biggest thing I ever boated, around thirteen feet, and two heavy for us to weigh, thousands of pounds.

"And this, me and my motor bike, about half-way across Australia. Those naked kids with the mops of tangled hair are aborigines, of course — aboes, as the back-country whites call them. I don't think they'd ever seen anyone arrive in their village on a motor bike before. I went all the way to the west coast, then north to Eighty Mile Beach, and back to Sydney by bus and train.

"But the best of it was stuff you couldn't photograph. Like the time on top of Mauna Loa at night. Naval of the world, you know, spitting fire all the time. It was erupting in a quiet, civilised kind of way, and I was standing there, looking into the fiery pit, when someone further along on the rim fell in — or much more likely *jumped* in, I'd say. Before I knew what was happening, here was this black body hurtling down into the cauldron of white-hot fire."

"What makes you think they jumped?"

"No scream. Not a sound. Just that black form, twisting a little, as it plunged to instant vaporization."

"You seem to have made the most of the tourist scene."

"But best of all was the fire walk."

"Fire walk? You mean a pit of red-hot rocks?"

"I've done it twice," Kirk said, "each time with a group of Polynesians, at the end of a long ceremony, all of us in a state of ecstasy or trance or whatever you'd call it — anyway, in an exalted psychic condition that completely protected us from the hot coals."

"Pity you don't have a photograph of that."

"Well, it isn't the sort of thing you can photograph very easily, unless you have a professional photographer in tow."

"I'd sure like to see it done," Jonathan said.

"Well, I can't offer you a fire walk, but how about a seance?"

"A seance! Talking to dead people through a medium?"

"Sure, if that's what you want. The spirits co-operate willingly."

"I thought that stuff went out with Mackenzie King."

"You'll find out different if you come along with me on Thursday night."

"OK," Jonathan agreed. "Why not?"

So, a few days later he went with Kirk to a private house, where they sat in a circle in a dimly-lit room, listening to a lot of bumps and noises and some vague voices.

"Anyone on the Other Side you'd like to contact?" the medium whispered.

"Sure," Jonathan said, "my dead brother Joel."

There were more bumps and noises and then a muffled voice, "This is your brother, Jonathan, speaking from the Other Side."

"Wow!" Jonathan exclaimed, "It's him! Any word from Mother?"

"We're together all the time," the muffled voice responded. "She's very happy."

The voices faded, and someone else spoke with a member of the spirit world. Later, he and Kirk discussed it briefly.

"Well, what did you think? Surprised, eh?"

"I'll say," Jonathan agreed. "Only, you see, I never had a brother, either dead or alive."

This didn't faze Kirk for a second. "Someone else then," he said. "You must have had someone who was just like a brother to you. "

"Yes, I did," Jonathan agreed. "Jamie Penchley. But he isn't dead, unless he died this week. He runs a real estate office in Black River New Brunswick."

"Someone else, then?"

"This guy has a doctorate," Jonathan reminded himself, "five years of postgraduate work, dozens of publications, a thesis in hard covers. And he believes in ghosts!"

He didn't put it to Kirk in those words, because he enjoyed yarning over the coffee machine, but ... well ... what was education for, if not to free you from myth and superstition? He supposed it was among people like Kirk that the Bible-Believing Scientists got their recruits. Then he wondered about the fire walk. Not much doubt that it really happened, but how? Did you have to believe a lot of nonsense to get into the psychic state that allowed you to walk safely through fire?

On one of his rare visits to the Faculty Club he shared a table with Charlie English whose eldest daughter had just got married in pomp and white satin, with the usual organ music and the usual attendants in rented suits, standing before a god in whom they didn't believe, making vows they didn't intend to keep.

"Costs thousands and thousands to marry off a daughter," Charlie complained. "Like those ski vacations the kids demanded after they'd won the downhill championships."

"Why do you do it?" Jonathan demanded.

"The skiing?"

"No, of course not. The weddings."

"Well, you've got to do *something* with your money."

"You could spend it protecting the environment, or helping people in the Third World get clean drinking water."

"Hell," Charlie laughed. "That wouldn't be any fun."

"Was that costume parade of a wedding fun?"

"No, I must admit it wasn't. And the reception wasn't much fun, either. But people expect it."

"Do they? I'll bet they're just as bored with the whole thing as you are."

"Maybe so. I guess the people who really enjoy weddings are the companies selling and renting all that junk you have to eat, drink and wear. And the photo studios."

"Yes. And I'll bet you'll go right ahead and do the same thing with your next daughter."

"Probably. It really is a big deal for the girls, I guess. And I must say I do enjoy the Alpine skiing. While I can. I'll be too old for it, soon."

"And then?"

"I don't know. Stay home and drink single malts, most likely."

Dr. Elizabeth Welty. A small, dark, intense woman. Unmarried. Hard worker. Took Can-Lit seriously. Published

New Criticism. Admired all the right things, including Can-Lit's Top Ten, living and dead.

"My trouble, John, is that I'm in a blind alley here; I've gone as far as they'll let me go. There's no way a woman will ever be Dean of Arts, or even head of a department."

"That's likely true, Liz, though things may change."

"Too late for me, if they do."

Dr. Welty didn't like being called "Liz" but she forgave Jonathan because he was one of the few people in the department who lent her a sympathetic ear. She really was having a difficult career. Ten years older than Jonathan, she published frequently in all the right places. Her papers were fresh enough to be quotable without being controversial. She certainly had the qualifications, and had she been a man she likely would have been Vice-Chair instead of Fitzgibbon. Occasionally Jonathan visited one of her classes and brought as much humour as he could to his lecture.

"A change from my approach," Dr. Welty told him. "I just don't have a funny bone in my body, unfortunately."

Jonathan tried to interest her in things outside the academic circle — women in politics, the plight of street kids in Halifax, polluted drinking water, cancer in the air — but when he tried it he could see her eyes going blank.

"I know it's a blind spot, John, but I'm not very interested in *people*. Scholarship has been my thing, ever since highschool."

"I've always thought people more important than books," Jonathan said.

"And, I must admit, I think books are more important. People come and go. Books go on forever. Literature is a great structure that grows richer and more complex with time."

"Perhaps society is, too."

"Perhaps. But I'll leave the problems of society to the experts who know what they're doing."

"You think some of them do?"

Jonathan refused absolutely to take part in campus politics. He'd never get ahead, he knew, without committee work, back-scratching, ass-kissing, petty scheming — but getting ahead didn't seem that important. He'd rather live and die an Associate Professor, he told himself, than waste his life like that.

"You just aren't cut out for an academic," Charlie English told him. "You ought to be doing some kind of field work, saving the world socially or biologically or whatever."

"I sure do think it needs saving," Jonathan agreed.

"And isn't that what politicians are for?"

"I suppose so. But they aren't doing their job, are they?"

"Maybe you should be in there pitching."

"Join one of those political parties, you mean? Help rig party conventions? Tie myself to the ass-end of some potential leader and work like hell to convince people he's the Second Coming?"

"I suppose that's about it," Charlie agreed. "The alternative is to work for Project Ploughshares or Greenpeace."

And so, more and more, he turned back to Sarah, who was not only wife and lover, but also one of his own tribe, still a mere teaching assistant, at the bottom of the academic totem pole. Only graduate students counted for less. But Sarah, like Jonathan, was pleased with her life as it was, not scrambling to get ahead. "If people want to get ahead, let them work at it," she said. "I don't even *like* the kind of society we have, much less trying to succeed in it. I'd prefer to live in a hunting and gathering culture to tell the truth."

"Where life is nasty, brutish, and short," Jonathan quoted. "O bosh!" she said. "What did Hobbes know about it? I've been reading social anthropology. The food-gathering cultures are among the happiest on earth. We just won't leave them be. We're bound and determined to make them miserable camp-followers of the American way of life."

Occasionally Jonathan brought one of his students to dinner. They were, of course, *his* camp-followers, and in most cases the visits were essentially meaningless. But with a young man named Ahab, Israeli by nationality, Palestinian by descent, there was something a bit more. When he left, Sarah commented: "He's in love with you, Jonathan. Anyone can see it."

"I wouldn't have thought it was that obvious."

"Well, it is — to me, anyway. And what about you?"

"What about ... you mean ...?"

"Yes."

"Well, of course not. You can see that too, can't you?"

"In a way. He's sort of special though, isn't he?"

"No more than several others — my disciples, the tiny band of my devoted acolytes. They sort of make up for the professors. There's hope, at least, for one or two of them. This boy is going to marry a Jew."

"Good God!"

"Not, of course, a Jewish wedding. They are Arab and Jew by descent, not by religion."

"I suppose there ought to be a lot more of it. But still..."

"And truly, honestly, I don't want to take any of them to bed with me."

"I don't think I'd be jealous, even if you did," she said. "See what an ego I have!"

Jonathan laughed. "Really, Sarah! You know perfectly well that I'm an incurable heterosexual monogamist."

"I don't believe there's any such animal," she retorted.

"Not even among women?" he teased.

"Especially not among women! But anyway, it isn't sex I'm talking about."

"No? Oh, I get it. It's like they say about the Inuit. It's not the woman you sleep with that counts. It's the one who tends your lamp."

This time she really laughed, grabbed him, and began having a mock fight.

"I love you," she said.

"Yes."

"Is that all you can say — 'yes?'"

"Yes to everything."

"You know," she said, "I find the students very compelling — so vulnerable, so easily hurt, so much in need of an older person's knowledge and wisdom."

"If the older person has any knowledge and wisdom," Jonathan interjected. "I often wonder if I do."

"And it's true," she added, "that some of them, young women as well as young men, come on to you in a rather intense emotional way. All too easy for teachers to get into trouble with them. I really feel sorry for the occasional man who gets caught off balance by a female student."

"It happens even oftener with male students, I'm sure," Jonathan said. "They come to their tutors, men or women, with love in their eyes. Unlike female students, they'd never complain about the attentions of a professor; to do so would be an admission of weakness and immaturity.

"I could well imagine someone like McMann, for instance, saying to such a boy, 'If you'd like to catch up, over the summer, on some of the reading you've missed, I've got a really quiet place on one of the Muskoka lakes — so isolated that you can sunbathe and swim in the nude.'"

"The boy would understand the invitation, of course. If he accepted it, the affair would be perfectly safe."

"And," Sarah added, "why not?"

"The academic board would surely regard it as unethical behaviour by the professor," he said.

"Oh I guess so — but nowadays they might tend to ignore it," she paused, reflecting. "You know, Jonathan, you've never told me much about your special friends."

"Well, you know about my girlfriends."

"Sure. But others. When you were growing up?"

"There was Jamie Penchley, of course. We grew up together, went to college at the same time, then studied different things, and ended up in different parts of the country — the usual story I guess. We were about as close as brothers, but there was no strong emotional tie."

"But with students you have emotional ties."

"Oh yes. Let me see. I had no brothers or sisters, but I always loved kids. Perhaps I loved them because my family was so sparse. I don't know."

"Yes. We'll soon have kids of our own," Sarah said. "Three, at least. Meanwhile, I suppose the students are your kids, so to speak."

"Sure, common enough, I guess. But I've always loved young children more than adults, even young adults. There've been a dozen or more very special kids in my life. Some are still my friends, though I don't see them oftener than once a year. Even when I was a teenager chasing my first girlfriends I'd meet a youngster — and right away the kid would be in my arms. Whether they were still in rompers, or starting junior high, they all seemed to know instinctively that I'd never turn them away."

"Are you saying kids have been your only friends?"

"Oh no, of course not, but my best friends, perhaps, and sometimes one of them was close enough to my own age to be a kid brother or sister. There was a little girl ... but no ... I'll tell you about Frankie. In my last highschool year I was walking down the corridor with a classmate when this kid came charging around a corner and almost crashed into us.

"Hey! Watch it, Frankie!" my friend said.

"'Sorry,' the boy said, and smiled broadly at us, and went on his way. Then he turned and looked back, and our eyes met. He was about thirteen, and beautiful in that special way of some Irish kids — blue eyes, dark curly hair, freckles across his nose, a kid you'd give your soul to own.

"'Seems like you know him,' I said.

"'Sure. Frankie Brennan. Magistrate Brennan's kid — lives down the street from me.'

"I soon discovered that this boy was a favourite with everybody — classmates, teachers, even older students. I kept seeing him around, seeing him with dancing eyes and high spirits, but I never spoke to him until one day I was sitting in the grandstand at the sport field watching a soccer game, and he came and sat right next to me.

"'Hi Frankie,' I said, and he moved in close. Then, a minute later, he did something really astonishing: he put an arm around my shoulders and hugged me, just for a second, and I turned toward him. His eyes, for once, were frightened. But I smiled, and his face lit up, and I reached over and took his hand, and he laced his fingers through mine. He'd been worshipping me from afar, you see, the way only a schoolchild can worship someone three years older — and there I was, with the most wonderful kid brother for the rest of that year — a kid as beautiful, and obliging, and loving, as any I'd ever known."

"What about your buddy Jamie Penchley? Wasn't he jealous?"

"Oh no. Not at all. The three of us often went camping and fishing together. Jamie and I took turns teaching him to use a canoe, and that winter the three of us went plunging down snow slopes on a toboggan. There were nights when the boy slept in my arms, head on my shoulder, days when we went swimming, or shared a bath, slippery with soap. Sometimes I helped with his lessons, and when I left in the evening he'd hug and kiss me, his mother or father standing by, delighted that he'd found an older friend, able to be of real use to him. His schoolwork improved, and his behaviour was simply perfect. We had a wonderful, playful relationship that lasted for many months, but of course it had to come to an end next autumn when I went off to college."

"Isn't it always that way with kids? I mean, it can't last, can it?"

"Well, it could if you were leading a really settled life, in one place — then the child could grow up with you, and you'd be adult friends — but not in North America, where you live in six different places between highschool and rest home.

"Four years later, when he came to St. John's, Frankie and I had lunch together and shared memories.

"'There were one or two teachers who were very good to me in highschool,' he said, 'but I never met another friend like you.'"

"That," said Sarah, "explains a lot about why I love you." She put her arms around Jonathan, and kissed him lightly on the cheek.

"Just the way Frankie used to do it," he laughed, and reached for her and took her into a deep embrace. "But there'll be no going separate ways for us."

"You bet there won't."

They went off to the bedroom and had a long delightful session of forepleasure, climax and after-pleasure.

Later, they talked more about it.

"There's a fine distinction between the way you love a child and the way you love your sexual partner," Jonathan said. "The hugs and kisses are really very much the same. Perhaps that's why there are so many tragic crossovers, so many people hungry for sex with kids."

"It's frightening even to think about it," Sarah said. "Real, unselfish love can be just a step away from the most horrible crime, right?"

"I suppose you could say that," Jonathan agreed, "but I think the step is really a very long one. The whole process of submerging yourself in the other person — of surrender — is a world apart from the feather-light touch of your love for a child. I can see how the tragedy happens, just the same."

She kissed him on the ear, and went off to make cocktails:

"Light ones, you know. Almost feather-light. Mustn't be surrendering and submerging ourselves in alcohol. Leave that for people who don't have the sur ... sub ..."

"Oh, shut up," Jonathan broke in, laughing.

Between a Sleep and a Sleep

Jonathan stirred heavily, reluctant to let go of slumber. Sarah was saying something ... something ... then the dream faded as her voice came clearly into his ear.

"It's started," she said.

He sat up, reached tor the light switch. It could be only one thing.

"Labour pains?"

"No. Amniotic fluid. The membrane has ruptured."

"Oh. Need a towel, or something?"

"Yes, please."

He padded, half awake, to the bathroom. The cold tiles of the floor brought him fully to his senses. He jumped back into bed beside Sarah, passing the towel. This, then was The Day. Very considerate of that baby, he reflected, to arrive during March break.

"Feel OK?"

"Yes, I feel fine. But once the amnion has broken, you know the baby is going to be born. What time is it?

He peered at his watch. "Just after three. Want me to turn the heat up a bit, maybe make coffee?"

"Sure. I'll just lie here for now. I can feel the baby moving a little. It hasn't been moving very much, lately, you know. But it is already in the birth position, head downwards."

"You sure?"

"Yes, I can tell. Some people can't, I guess. But I can feel exactly the way the baby is lying."

Jonathan, who never wore pyjamas, and didn't own a bathrobe or slippers, picked some clothes off the floor, got socks out of a drawer, and dressed. It was chilly. On his way to plug in the electric kettle, he turned up the heat. He could hear wind moaning softly around the eaves, snow batting against the windows — a blizzard in the making, perhaps.

This rented house was not exactly the sort of thing he would have built himself; it served its purpose, that was all — tiled floors, fake fireplace, small electric range. He set a pot of coffee to brewing, and sat in the kitchen, worrying. A damn poor day for a home birth if anything happened to go wrong, he reflected. What if the roads were closed? What if ... would they send a helicopter? Can helicopters fly in blizzards? Stop your nonsense! he told himself firmly. Sarah knows what she's doing. But still ... Too late to change anything now. They'd made their decision months ago — or, to be more accurate, Sarah had made it. The baby would be born at home, today, without medical assistance.

"Without *any* assistance," he told himself, "except what I can give — whatever that may be." The ordeal was at hand — the ordeal he'd been trying not to face. You can't quarrel with your pregnant wife, he told himself, even if quarrelling would do any good, but Sarah wasn't going to change because of anything he might say. He'd worried over her, couldn't stand the thought of her running needless risks. And then (he had to admit it) he'd worried about himself. If something did go wrong, surely he'd be held responsible. Well ...

The coffee was ready, and Sarah came out of the bathroom, adorable in her lilac-coloured bathrobe. She had spread quite a bit across the hips, but, unlike so many women in late pregnancy, wasn't enormously big in front.

"I'm lucky," she'd told him. "I have a loosely-articulated pelvis." Where did she get that? he wondered.

"Feeling OK?"

"Yes, of course. How about you?"

"A little shaky," he admitted. "I wish we'd prepared for it more — I don't know, taken lessons, or something."

"Nobody needs lessons to become a mother, darling. All you've got to do is let it happen."

"Well ... if you'd gone to a gynecologist ... or even a family doctor ...

"We don't have a family doctor, remember? We're never sick, and nobody needs a doctor when they're well. If there was anything wrong with me I'd know about it, and go to a clinic."

"Yes, I guess you would — but I can't help being nervous."

"That's OK. It's a big event — at least for the woman — the biggest thing since she was born herself. But pregnancy isn't a disease, and birth isn't a medical crisis."

"Still no pains?"

"Slight contractions. No pains yet. why don't you go back to bed? It's awfully early, and this may take all day. I'd rather sit up, myself."

"Me too. I couldn't possibly sleep."

"See what's on the all-night radio, then. Acid rock, I bet, this time of the morning."

The music came floating from the speaker. King Crimson — nice, gentle stuff.

Time slipped by — didn't drag, as he would have expected. Jonathan made toast. They sat eating it, listening to the plaintive strains of flute and oboe. He was surprised to see by his watch that it was 4:30 already. Then Sarah bit down a little harder on her toast, sat up straight and sudden.

"That's it," she said, "the first hard contraction. Not as strong as I expected. Not really painful. But there's no mistake about it."

"What's it feel like, exactly?"

"Well ..." she smiled at him (brave, he thought) "it's rather like a muscle cramp, a kind of seizure that you can't control. But not painful — at least, not yet. I expect it would become painful if you tried to fight it."

"You keep hearing that labour pains are absolute agony," he said.

"Perhaps they are, for a lot of people. Many women are in pretty poor shape, right from birth, and many others are badly out of condition. Not me. I was swimming and diving at the university pool less than a month ago. I've been cross-country skiing. I walked about five miles through the woods and along the lake shore just yesterday.

Jonathan recalled a story from childhood: "Old woman I knew," he said, "claimed she dug three barrels of potatoes the day her first kid was born." He paused, reflecting. "And you hear that Indian women — the ones out in the bush — don't have a hard time with their births."

"That's because they have to work," Sarah said decisively — "pretty hard, too, most of them, right up to a few hours before the delivery — no time to sit around with their feet up, getting fat. I've even heard that when a native band in the north is on the move the woman only begins to lag behind when labour starts. Then her mother or sister or some other woman stays with her. And afterwards they take the baby in a back pack and hurry to catch up with the others."

"Sounds incredible," Jonathan commented, "but I suppose it's true."

Time slipped by. There was a second, and a third contraction. And a fourth.

Sarah seemed to know exactly what she wanted, Jonathan reflected, even though this was a wholly new experience for her. But she'd had a lot of moral support and advice from the feminists in Women's Studies. It had been a long time before he agreed to a home birth, and he kept trying, one way and another, to simplify it, to dodge responsibility.

First he'd phoned a doctor.

"Talk to her gynecologist," the doctor said, "and take his advice."

Several other doctors. Not one of them would attend a home birth, except in a crisis. One that seemed a little more sympathetic than the others explained that he'd want oxygen standing by, and a blood pressure monitor to keep track of things second by second, just in case the pressure began to drop. There could be internal bleeding, you know. And anyway, he'd want a report from her gynecologist, everything from blood sugar levels to a guarantee that there was no danger of septicaemia.

"Septicaemia!" Sarah had exclaimed. "Is he nuts? I'm not sick!"

"I guess they want to be within reach of emergency equipment in case they need it," Jonathan reasoned, "even if it's only one chance in a hundred."

"Bullshit!" she said. "They want you in a delivery room, with your legs up in stirrups, shot full of drugs so you won't give them any trouble, all hair shaved off, and washed with disinfectant. And more than likely they'll want to open you up with a scalpel. What do they call it? A pissiotomy? And then they sew you up afterwards with monofiliment. That's what they want to do."

Getting no advice from doctors, Jonathan had turned to friends. One of them, who kept a natural foods store, gave him a thick volume in paperback called *Our Bodies Ourselves*. Advice to women, including natural childbirth. Told about exercise. Told about correct attitudes. Quoted statistics showing home births were healthier, for the baby, than those in hospitals. But told you absolutely nothing about actual procedures.

What was the "birth attendant," as they liked to call it, supposed to do, apart from giving moral support? That, apparently, was very important. But what else? A midwife would be expected to know, of course, but the reader isn't a midwife. What's even meant by "tying off the cord?" Tying *how* exactly? Some animals bite it off, don't they? But that must be much later. Otherwise, why do you tie it? Must be to stop bleeding. All very puzzling. Do you have to hold the baby up by its feet and slap its bottom to make it breathe? Apparently doctors do that. He'd seen it in photographs.

"That's when they've filled the mother full of drugs," Sarah told him. "The baby isn't breathing because it has been knocked out with sedatives. That's why."

Jonathan fretted. What if the birth is difficult? How soon do you reach inside and try to pull the head forward? If there is a head. What if it hasn't turned as it should? What if ...?

"Stop worrying, Jonathan," Sarah told him. "Pregnancy isn't a disease. If something was going wrong I'd know it. I'm in touch with my own body, darling. Ninety-five chances in a hundred the birth will be perfectly normal, and I'll *know* that it is."

"Still, most everyone goes to a hospital."

"That's changing. In normal births hospitals can only do damage — trying to hurry things along, trying to ease the contractions, trying one drug or another, forceps all ready to squeeze the baby's head out of shape if they think it isn't coming fast enough."

"I suppose that's true," he'd agreed reluctantly.

"That's not all," she said. "The minute it's born they haul it away, and of course it yowls for its mother, so they feed it on sugar water. *Sugar water!* And they drop silver nitrite into its eyes, just in case you've had the clap."

The last week or so, when the baby was "overdue" according to conventional wisdom (counting forward from Sarah's last menstruation), she'd insisted that this, too, was nonsense. "Don't fret," she said. "The baby isn't overdue at all. The baby will know when it's ready to be born."

That seemed to be right, Jonathan reflected. Pregnancy doesn't begin with the last menstruation. They knew when

Sarah had her fertile periods, and today, as it happened, was exactly nine months and nine days from the middle of her last ovulation, two hundred and eighty-one days, to be exact. That wasn't overdue at all. It was right on time.

Jonathan sighed heavily. He'd grown up in an outport, after all, surrounded by domestic animals, and not one of them that he knew of had died giving birth. Sarah must know what was good for her. Didn't she eat wheat germ every day? Take vitamins? Even folic acid, whatever that was. But he wished, fervently, the whole thing was over, or that they were no more than two blocks from the nearest hospital, instead of thirty miles, with a snowstorm blowing up into a blizzard. He had already magnified the blowing snow into a "living storm" as his fishermen-neighbours used to call it. The roads might be blocked for three days.

Would there be a snowmobile?

At 6:15 Sarah began pacing the floor.

"I guess this is what they call the second stage of labour," she said. "The contractions are stronger, and you can see they're coming closer together."

Jonathan was getting more and more fidgety. Last night's dishes were piled beside the sink. He decided to wash them.

"Oh," Sarah said, "there's something else you can do. Take all the clothes off the bed, and cover it with a plastic sheet."

Oh yes. For the blood!

He stripped and covered the bed, and came back to the kitchen. He filled the sink with hot water, working up a lather with the old soap saver in which scraps of laundry soap were imprisoned in their little wire cage. He slid the dishes into the water.

"I'm going to take a shower," Sarah said, and headed for the bathroom.

He dipped a hand into the water. Almost scalding hot, he decided, and dried his hands on a tea towel.

"On second thought, there may not be time for that shower," Sarah said, reappearing in the kitchen. "I'll go lie down. I'll call you when I need you."

The water cooled a bit, and Jonathan slid his hands into it, mopping the dishes. One by one he began transferring them to the board where they would drain. Just then there was a sort of yelp from the adjoining bedroom — not a cry of pain exactly, more like a cry of startled surprise. He rushed toward the bedroom, dripping dishwater.

"You OK?"

"Yes," she gasped, breathing heavily. "Quite OK. But perhaps you'd better come in ... *now*." The last word was almost a squeak. She gave a sort of gasp as another contraction put all her trunk muscles into spasm.

Jonathan rushed out to dry his hands, rushed back to the bedside. Sarah was lying wide-eyed as though looking into starless space, in the same position as before. He could see the lips of the vulva spread into an expanding circle, pubic hair stretched above, a round object pressing outward. It took him a moment to realize that the round object was the crown of a tiny head. A second later, it slipped out.

"Is ... is it born?" Sarah asked weakly.

"Just the head," he reported.

She gathered her strength. "Hold me up," she said. He put a pillow behind her. Then she bore down heavily with the muscles of her abdomen. At the same moment, Jonathan slipped his hands under the tiny shoulders and drew the baby gently towards him. And there it was, lying between its mother's legs, already drawing its first breath, mewing like a kitten. It was a sort of bluish-pink. Was that normal? Was this what they called a blue baby? He didn't know. There were volumes of things he didn't know. Volumes!

"The cord," he said. "It's around the baby's neck." It was, in fact, wrapped around the small neck twice. But the baby was breathing, so it couldn't be all that tight.

"Don't stretch it," Sarah warned. She sat up straighter. "Just lift the baby, will you? Gently, now. It's a girl."

He picked up the baby, holding her head-down between Sarah's legs, and turned her whole body twice to unwind the cord. Sarah lay back. He placed the baby on her belly. He was surprised and relieved that there wasn't any blood, or almost none: just a little semi-clotted stuff that had followed the baby out of the birth canal — no real bleeding. He discovered suddenly that he was breathing heavily, like he'd been running. Sarah seemed relaxed, almost sleepy.

He realized that she hadn't ordered any boiling water. What's all this, he thought, about the gallons and gallons of hot water that doctors in books always order to he ready — or the midwife, or whoever is helping with the birth? What on earth is it for? Is it just part of the mystification? part of the ritual surrounding something as simple as this?

He noticed that the ring was still on his finger. He hadn't had time to take it off. The cord was still pulsing, like a heart beat. Wait a couple of minutes, and the cord will collapse by itself. He knew *that* much, had heard it somewhere; no need to rush things. Sure enough, the last few squirts passed into the baby's body, and the cord collapsed, its work done. No sign of the placenta, yet.

He went to the bathroom, came back with dental floss and scissors.

"Tie it as close to her belly as you can," Sarah told him. "Then tie it again, a couple of inches away."

He put in a pair of reef knots, tying them tight, then snipped the cord between them, with scissors. As he did this, he noticed that his hands were trembling. He picked up the baby, and felt a sudden rush of ... of what? Not adrenalin, for sure. Something else, something like intense emotion, like tenderness and awe mingled together, something as deep and moving as first love. God! This must be the "bonding" that they talked about, the sense of magic that even the father experienced with his first child, especially if he actually assisted with its birth. It was worth far more than all the worry, the anxiety, to experience such a ... he groped for a word ... such an *epiphany* as this!

He decided the baby needed a wash, to get rid of those bits and pieces of amniota sticking to her skin. As he picked her up, she gave a lusty cry, not so much like a mewing kitten as like one demanding its mother, in distress. He laid her on Sarah's breast, and she began to suck, though of course there'd be no milk, as yet. She was contented, though. It wasn't milk she wanted, but a mouthful of her mother's breast. Oral eroticism in the just-born?

"It's like dawning, isn't it?" Sarah said. "Like darkness passing away. Like the sun bursting out of a cloud."

"All that and much more!" he agreed.

"I'm glad you feel it too," she said.

"A miracle forever renewed!"

"Lord, aren't we a pair of hacks with our clichés!"

"A new principle for my English classes," he laughed. "All really great emotion can be expressed only in clichés. I must remember that one."

Jonathan went to the bathroom and filled the basin with water barely warm to the touch. The baby would be used to body heat, and that would be the right temperature for her first bath. As he picked her up she whimpered a little, but became quiet as he immersed her in the warm water, gently sponging off the scraps of white tissue that clung like wet cotton batting to every crease of her skin. She was turning pinker by the minute, he noted, no longer with that bluish tint. Perhaps this was what happened when she began breathing, charging her blood with higher levels of oxygen than she'd been used to in the womb.

Aren't you supposed to wash out their mouths? he wondered. Well, sometimes, perhaps. Obviously this baby wasn't choking on amniotic tissue. He picked her up and wrapped her in a towel, patted her dry, discarded the towel, held her against his left shoulder. She began sucking at his shirt. He felt a clutching at his heart. Jonathan had known many children, from toddlers up to undergraduates. He'd loved many of them. But this child, he was certain, was going to be special in a very special way.

We'll call her after Sarah's mother, if Sarah agrees, he decided. We'll name her Judith.

Sarah was sitting up.

"Placenta still hasn't separated, apparently."

"Maybe I should call a doctor and ask about it," he offered.

"Oh, I don't know. Wait a little while. There's no bleeding or anything. No pain. I think I'll go to the bathroom. What time is it?"

Jonathan had forgotten about the time. He glanced at his watch.

"Just seven-thirty."

"Oh," Sarah said. "I completely lost track of time. It could be a few minutes, or it could be hours and hours. It's like you're taken over absolutely by the process. Time stops. Anyway, I'm going to the bathroom. I've been lying here long enough."

A minute later he heard the toilet flush.

"Well, that's that," she announced. "It's down the drain where it belongs."

"You mean the afterbirth?" he called.

She laughed. "Yes, dear, the afterbirth. What did you think I was talking about?"

Jonathan was still carrying the baby, a towel around her for warmth. She had stopped sucking his shirt, and had gone to sleep on his shoulder. The wind howled, The snow beat against the windows. Everything was beautiful.

"I'm going to make some coffee," Sarah said. "I'm hungry, too."

"Then I'll make some scrambled eggs," he offered. "What about the baby?"

"If you lay her down quietly she'll likely stay asleep."

Pause. He kissed his wife on the back of the neck as she bent over the coffee machine.

"I thought you might like to name her Judith."

"Well, sure, if that suits you. It's a pretty name, but it's dignified, too."

Long pause. Scrambled eggs piled on a plate. Coffee steaming in mugs.

"So it's all over?" Jonathan was incredulous.

"No dear, it's just beginning. A whole new life for both of us. And in a few days we can begin intercourse again. How long has it been since last time?"

"Five days, I think. No. Six."

"They used to believe you had to stop during pregnancy. Doctors even *ordered* you to."

"Well," Jonathan mused, "I suppose if a man actually lay on your belly it mightn't be good. Was that the reason?"

"I think it was just nonsense, like so much of the stuff they told you."

Pause. "Will Judith need something? Water maybe?"

"I'll let her suck again, when she wakes up. There'll be milk as soon as she needs it."

And of course there was.

The Birth of Magic

When Judith was two and a half years old her parents, Sarah and Jonathan, took her to Newfoundland for the summer. It was the first of many such visits, and she fell instantly in love with The Rock, as Newfoundlanders like to call their beautiful island. She loved the fog, the rains, the wet sunshine that appeared between showers, the silvery capelin that came piling up on beaches by the millions, the carpets of lichens that covered The Barrens between the blueberry bushes, and the deep sphagnum moss on the bogs between the glowing red caps of the bakeapples.

Newfoundland created her first lasting memories. She had been to coastal British Columbia the year before, but remembered nothing of that, even a year later. Memories of that first Newfoundland experience remained with her for the rest of her life. She recalled trifles, and brought them out from time to time like jewels from an old box: the shocking chill of the sea water when she waded out among the teeming capelin, the crunch-crunch of the reindeer moss under bare feet in dry weather, and the silky droop of the same plant when the fog rolled in, the drumming and rumbling of the surf through the bedroom window in the long twilight of the early summer night.

Mud trout, as they are called, brought home by one of her cousins (actually a second cousin, but outport people rarely bother with such distinctions) gently cooked to pink perfection and carefully deboned by Mother revealed to her for the first time the magical flavour of this small, rare fish.

A great swell from a distant storm at sea piled shoreward against walls of basalt rock, spouting sky-high in roars of thunder, and taught her to feel the awesome power of nature. She saw gulls soar on motionless wings, moving without effort above the line of the cliff, and Jonathan had to explain to her that the wind, blowing shoreward from the sea, turned upwards when it met the cliff, and supported the gulls so that they did not need to flap like songbirds, but could glide along, gently sinking through the air as the air itself moved up around them.

She sat on a wharf and watched boys jigging conners — the fish kicking furiously as they were hoisted out of the water, landed on the planks of the wharf, and had the hooks jerked ruthlessly out of their mouths, while a boy's foot held them in place. It was brutal and fascinating. The image would remain with her, though she was not quite old enough to feel sorry for the fish. Sometimes they would be chopped up for bait, sometimes thrown back, damaged, into the water, sometimes left gasping in the sunshine, to expire slowly, and finally to be food for a passing gull. Those same boys, who seemed so cruel when fishing for sport, would play with Judith, or with any other small child, and would be as gentle as lambs.

In a sandy cove out of sight of the village she saw them dashing naked into the surf, whooping and hollering. One of them helped her off with her playsuit, took her on his shoulders, and carried her out into the breakers. The spray blew over them, stinging and chilling her small body, and she squealed, half with pleasure and half with fright. Then the boy took her back to the beach and buried her up to her neck in the hot sand. Sometimes her parents were with her on those thrilling adventures, sometimes not. So long as she was with a group of outport children, they believed she'd be perfectly safe. Even if she fell out of a boat, they'd fish her out of the water unharmed, as they had done with other children many times before.

Dogs were everywhere, running free (she had rarely seen dogs roaming at will before) and she mingled with them on equal terms. They seemed to accept her as a sort of superior puppy, and were well aware that they, too, were responsible for her safety.

In this village dogs were almost honourary people — a status accorded to no other animal except, very rarely, to one of the Newfoundland ponies who happened to have a kind and thoughtful owner. Those horses were rather special, too: small and rugged, gentle and friendly, and hardly required to do any work at all. They sometimes cantered around with boys riding them bareback (Judith, too, got to ride a pony, one of the older boys holding her securely in front of him) but that wasn't work — it was just a game for horses and kids to play together.

The ancestors of those little horses had been hard-working animals, had ploughed many a potato garden, hauled rock on "stone boats" when their owners were clearing land, drew firewood on catamaran sleds from the forests beyond The Barrens, brought loads of capelin from the beaches to fertilize the cabbage patches, and often felt the sting of a switch across their hind quarters, but nowadays little was expected of them beyond foraging for a living in woods and abandoned fields. Some people lamented that the breed was dying out, but at least the survivors were having a pleasant time of it.

Judith saw a goose followed by a flock of goslings, five of them, in the back yard, growing fat, their yellow down gradually mixed with darker strands. Then one morning a gosling was dead. She and Jonathan dug a grave for it, and buried it under a lilac bush. It was her first experience of death.

"Little goose will never grow up, never have babies of her own," she said.

"No," Jonathan agreed. "Its life was very short, but it had a good time, and now it's over. People are like that too. Some of them never grow up."

"Will I grow up?"

"Yes. Almost certainly. Children in our part of the world don't die very often. In some countries they do, but not in Canada."

She went with Sarah and Jonathan to St. John's and Cape St. Francis, and saw the icebergs — floating fairyland castles as big as islands, with blue and green towers, and with blue caverns in their sides. It would be some years before Judith saw icebergs again, for they don't arrive every summer, but she kept talking about them, and made up her first story, a year or so later, about floating away on an iceberg to the land of the seals.

"Your bum would freeze on to the ice," Jonathan assured her.

"It wouldn't. I'd wear my snow suit," she said.

"How would you steer the icebergs?" Jonathan asked.

"I'd have a sail, of course. Anyone'd know that!"

He was pleased. A mind of her own at three and a half.

Her parents took her in a car to Ferryland, and there she saw fish being made in the old fashioned way — salted and cured in the sun. Men and women worked together spreading the half-dry slabs of codfish on trestles covered with chicken wire — there seemed to be miles and miles of those "flakes." The chicken wire was a modern improvement over the boughs that had been used on the drying flakes for hundreds of years. Otherwise it was the same as it had always been — the endless hand labour of the shore cure that produced the choicest kind of dried fish — spreading it, turning it, protecting it from sunburn, yaffling it and spreading it again, covering it quickly if rain started: and all this work after it had already been split and salted, stacked, pressed, washed out, pressed again. The result was such a rare product that you could never find it nowadays in a grocery store, golden and aromatic, and just right for fish and brewis. Virtually all the cured fish that you could buy was now made in drying machines, heavily salted, white, and only faintly echoing the flavour of the ancient shore cure that West Country fishermen of old England had perfected back in the days of the Tudor monarchs.

Judith knew nothing of this, of course, but her father knew all about it, and told it to her like a bedtime story. That was one of the things she forgot, but somehow or other, years later, she seemed to know about it when she saw people "making" small quantities of fish for their private use — "eating fish" as they called it, taking the kind of care they would never take with anything they made for the merchants.

Here, too, she went out with a crew of fishermen in a trap boat: a big, open skiff with an inboard motor, and a well, or hold, forward of the engine, for carrying loads of fish. She saw a cod trap "dried up" by men working in boats, hauling the net inboard until there was a struggling mass of codfish right at the surface of the water. Then, with dipnets, they transferred the fish to the bigger boat until the well was filled, and the boat's gunwales were only a few inches above the water.

"Ye are a real mascot, little maid," one of the fishermen told her. "Ye've brought us luck, for sure — best haul of fish we've had the summer — have to sign ye on as one o' the crew!"

The big boat went churning back to the fish wharf, and there the fish were tossed up to the pounds with two-pronged pitchforks, just like the ones in old pictures of His Satanic Majesty, the devil. The men had to be careful not to damage the fish with the tines. They speared them through the heads, because the heads, of course, would be discarded by the splitters, some parts of them salvaged by boys and by an army of stray cats.

Later she saw the boys cutting out the tongues, and sometimes the jowls as well, these being the very choicest parts of a fresh codfish. Still later, she shared a meal of tongues fried in butter — a dish that everyone agreed was among the choicest gifts of the sea, more robust than shrimp, more flavourful than oysters.

They drove back past Cape Race to St. Mary's Bay and the long road north to Colinet. They passed through forest and over barren ground, and, at one point, had to stop and wait for a herd of caribou, hundreds of animals, crossing the road like cattle.

In mid-summer they went to the bogs where the bakeapples grow, and filled buckets with the hard red drupes of this rare northern fruit. In just a few days the bakeapples ripened, turned soft and yellow, and were eaten with sugar and cream — Devonshire cream, collected from scalded milk, the only kind known in the outports. Even better, perhaps, were bakeapples made into jam — a confection with a flavour like nothing else on earth, beloved beyond all reason by Newfoundlanders.

"A food fit for the gods," Jonathan declared.

"I don't think they're quite as good as strawberries," Sarah said.

"A mere Mainland opinion," Jonathan retorted. "A bakeapple is to a strawberry as caviar is to a clam."

Later there were buckets brimming with blueberries to be taken back to Ontario, where one of Jonathan's colleagues was a famous wine maker who knew how to turn Newfoundland blueberries into a wine very much like Burgundy.

The birth of magic in a child's soul. It would colour all her life.

"Perhaps," Sarah said, "she'll be an artist or something — a poet, a music maker — who knows?"

"Let's not start planning her future," Jonathan said. "We have no business trying to shape her life. And remember the old adage, 'Blessed are they who expect nothing, for they will not be disappointed.'"

"That sounds cynical. But OK. I certainly wouldn't want to guide her into a career where she wouldn't be happy."

"We've both read the *Tao-teh-King*. Let's take it to heart. Especially where children are concerned. The less you *strive*, the more you'll accomplish."

"That's a rule of life that sounds very simple, but is really very difficult to apply."

It was the magic summer — no doubt about that — and on the way back to dim, dull, boring Ontario, where nobody lives by choice, but only for pay, little Judith begged for more of it:

"Jonathan, can we go back?"

"Of course, pet. But not till next summer. That's a long, long time from now, but we'll go. We'll go every year we can."

Judith accepted this. She had really no concept of how far off "next summer" might be, but children don't mind living on promises, especially when they know from experience that the promise will be kept.

The Lonely Sea and the Sky

The sea seemed to stretch out to the curve of the earth, the horizon a bow edged by a very thin band of white light. Faintly visible against it were the masts and bridges of ships, hull-down, headed south. From his vantage on the edge of the cliff Jonathan could just see them (what were they — thirty miles away?) like stitching on the edge of the sky. They were following the great circle route, he supposed, from northern Europe to Cape Cod. Here they were close to shore because the great circle, which he had traced on a globe when still a child, actually cut through the Island of Newfoundland. They gave the shore a respectable berth because of the dangers that had destroyed so many ships in the past — reefs, fogs, onshore currents setting toward Cape Race. It was many years now since a ship had foundered at Chance Cove or Cape Ballard or Mistaken Point, but they were still cautious, remembering the ghosts of drowned sailors that haunted that shore.

There were worse things than drowning, Jonathan mused. One of them might be the sense of futility that lay like dry rot at the heart of his generation. It might not be so everywhere, but in North America it was pervasive.

He watched a small ship, a two-masted coasting schooner under sail, come around the headland to the south, tacking into the offing, seeking sea room for a run down the coast. He had watched such ships ever since he had first walked the cliff paths, and he never saw one beating to windward without the feeling that he ought to be on her deck, directing her progress, guiding her through storm and calm to her safe destinations, or perhaps at the wheel, not in charge of the voyage, but watching that the sails drew properly, that the course was steady, keeping her close to the wind, helping her shoulder her way through the sea.

"I'd have made a good ship's master," Jonathan thought. "It's in my blood — or, as they say nowadays, in my genes."

Ten, fifteen generations of sailors stretched behind him, perhaps many more. His grandfather had sailed to Brazil and Portugal and Italy and Greece with loads of fish, and had never lost a ship in a long lifetime of command. For many generations his ancestors had been sailors and fishermen and shipbuilders. Some of them had doubtless put to sea to defeat Julius Caesar the first time the Romans attacked Britain. Some had perhaps guided Pytheas to Norway and Iceland three centuries before Caesar was born. His father, so far as he knew, had been the first of his family to stay on shore, measuring out dry goods for a merchant and, later, speeding cable messages across the ocean, because his mother hated the sea.

Women! he reflected. But then reflected further: no fun being a grass widow to a ship or a real widow to the sea, pacing around one of those glassed-in "widow's walks" on the roof of a seaman's house, gazing at the unforgiving ocean. A few women, captains wives, sailed with their men

— a very few. Some even gave birth to children at sea, the captain himself doing whatever he could as midwife. That took a special kind of courage, on the man's part as well as the woman's, but think how splendid it would be, to deliver your own child at sea!

Something less than a whisper stirred the grass beside his ear, and without warning Sarah was standing there, her foot almost touching his cheek. Sarah — friend, companion, lover — had a gift for moving silently through brush and wild flowers. This time she had stolen softly through the blue bellflowers that bloomed so abundantly along the cliff edge — Scotch bluebells, some people called them.

"You look like you're ready to venture out to the ends of the earth," she said. "You remember the line in the school books: 'I will arise and go, now?'"

"That was to an island in a lake," Jonathan said. "The islands I want to visit are asleep under alien stars."

"'A heaven all strange with tawny stars, and monstrous with an alien moon' — wasn't that another line from school?"

"Something like that, but it's romantic nonsense, you know. On my one long foreign voyage as a boy I learned that the stars don't change colour; the moon looks the same, no matter where you are."

'If you're near enough to a city it might be red from air pollution," Sarah suggested.

"I suppose it might. Let's just sit here a while ... I've been thinking I'd have made a good sailor."

"You *are* a good sailor."

"Oh, pleasure boats! That's not the same thing at all."

"Didn't Conrad say that yachtsmen were the best sailors in the world?"

"Yes. Something like that. In one or his last essays, when he realized that sailing ships had no future in world trade."

"But isn't it true?"

"Yes, technically, I suppose. But that's like comparing a sport hunter to an Indian who hunts for a living. The sport hunter with his telescopic sight may be a better shot, but it's the meat hunter who deserves respect."

"So how come you made just that one long voyage with your grandfather?"

"At first, I suppose, it was my father, who wanted something different for me — something really respectable in a suit and tie. Fathers always think they know what their sons ought to do."

"And later?"

"Well ... one thing after another. You know how it is."

"Yes ... I know. Women do it too — keep putting something off until it's too late."

"That one voyage I made as a young boy, to Gibraltar, and back by way of the West Indies, sailing with the westerlies across the North Atlantic, then southwest with the trade winds — I loved it. But of course a boy on his grandfather's ship is practically a passenger. And the bo'sun, a kind, good-looking, very young man, treated me as his special pet — made me climb to the masthead, slide down stays, taught me to tie a bowline, and things like that. He watched over me like a hen with a lone chick."

"Boys at sea often had a hard time of it, didn't they?"

"Oh yes. There was even a school of thought that ill-treatment was good for them. Sometimes they were kicked around, beaten, buggered. On some ships, that is."

"But you enjoyed it."

"Grandfather's ship was nothing like that. He had a voice like a foghorn, but he wouldn't harm a fly, or stand for any bullying on his ship. His mate did most of the navigation, and his bo'sun — funny, I've forgotten the man's last name — he let me call him Cy — must have been Cyrus-someone-or-other. It was only later, looking back, that I realized how he must have loved me. If your grandfather is the captain you can't hang around with him all the time, you know, but a boy can hang on the bo'sun's coat tails if he wants. If I'd made a few voyages with a man like Cy I could have been second mate in a trading ship by the age of eighteen, and a captain by the age of thirty."

"Then we never would have met."

"That's likely true. Makes you believe in the guiding hand of God, doesn't it?"

Jonathan lay with his head on Sarah's lap, and thought about clouds as sails.

The sails, the spars, the rigging rose toward the clouds in an uninterrupted procession, tapering upward in symmetrical billows.

"A sailing ship," his grandfather had told him, "is the most beautiful thing ever created by man."

His grandfather would have been thinking of a full-rigged ship, like the wonderful American clipper, the *Flying Cloud*, square-rigged on three masts, a queen of the high seas, but Jonathan, perversely, always preferred the tern schooners of a slightly later age, slender, graceful, usually painted white, with great sweeps of fore-and-aft sails that looked like the wings of giant birds.

This was such a ship, small by trans-ocean standards, but to Jonathan on his first voyage it was magnificent beyond words. There was a poem they'd had in school:

"Whither, O splendid ship, thy white sails crowding ..." He couldn't remember any more of it, and anyway the words didn't begin to do justice to the reality. He guessed that it had been written not by a man on a deck, but by a man at a desk.

The ship, shaping her sails to the wind, bending and recovering, moving onward in near silence, only the slap and hiss of waves along her sides and the creaking of the rigging to betray her motion, hardly needing even a guiding hand to her rudder, was as near to a living creature as anything made of wood and canvas could ever become. It was quite possible, he realised, to love a ship in a way that no one could ever love a house, or any other object made by hands.

Jonathan never did suffer seasickness. Perhaps the "civil" weather at the beginning of the voyage had something to do with it, letting him get inured to the rolling and pitching gradually, but he liked to think that his immunity came from his family, from ancestors who had gone to sea for untold centuries. "Shouldn't wonder," his grandfather said once, "if our folks was fishing off Cornwall when the Phoenicians sailed up there fer loads o' tin."

In May they sailed out of a snow squall into the Gulf Stream, and summer. It would go on being summer for a long time, since they didn't expect to return until late in July: Gibraltar, Trinidad, possibly New Orleans. Jonathan at twelve years of age carried the map of the world in his head, and knew its great ports by name. Even such places as Pernambuco and Malacca, hardly even names to landsmen, were woven intimately into the yarns he'd heard around the kitchen range when he was whittling his first toy boat.

The ship entered the Gulf Stream two days after leaving port. You could *see* the change in the ocean, which turned from gray to blue along a well-marked line, and was suddenly almost tropical. The weather grew much warmer, the wind came up with a brisk sea running from the southeast, and warm water started sloshing through the scuppers. Then the sailors took off their jackets and guernseys, left their sea boots below, and worked barefoot on deck. To Jonathan it was all a lark, like the day school got out, but he soon discovered that going barefoot wasn't entirely for fun: it was much safer than leather-soled boots, especially on wet decks, and he soon got used to the feeling of ropes and cross-trees under his feet. This was where his friend the bo'sun came in — forcing him to race up the rigging, scolding him if he hesitated, teaching him not only to obey orders instantly, without question, but to rely on himself, believe in himself, and above all never to hesitate because he was afraid.

The inheritor of a great tradition of seafaring — not just a few generations, but thousands of years of accumulated wisdom, some of it mere superstition, much of it the difference between life and death at sea — Jonathan had been absorbing sailor's lore quite unconsciously from the time he took his first steps. He could barely remember his grandfather teaching him the compass before he had learned to read (Nothe be East, No-Nothe East, Nothe East be Nothe, Nothe East) teaching him to recite the names of the great capes along the shores of the North Atlantic (Cape Race, Cape Sable, Cape Cod, Cape Hatteras). When had it all happened? Was he three years old? Four? And how much else had he absorbed in those days? So far as he could tell, no one had ever taught nim to handle a tiller, to bring the bow of a boat up against an approaching wave, to let it fall off in a following sea so the water didn't come over the stern, to guide its course by distant landmarks. His grandfather had shown him how to tie a reef knot instead of the "granny" knot that seemed to come natural to a child's hands, but when it came to actually reefing a boat's sail he seemed to know how to do it without being taught. Perhaps he had picked it up before he could read, learning it from pictures of reef points and reefed sails, for his grandparents' house was filled with pictures of ships — of stately schooners on a summer sea sailing past erupting volcanoes, painted by Italian artists and sold to ships' captains at Naples — pictures of clippers under full sail, leaning across the wind and tossing foam from their bows, pictures of huge trading ships with dozens of sails, including skys'ils and stu'ns'ils, spread to a following breeze. There were many things he didn't know, of course, things like how to tack a ship under full sail, how to "wear around" in a heavy wind, things like which sails to brace and which to loose, and just when to do it. Though it all made sense once you figured it out, it was a set of skills learned on the job, the skills of a mate or a captain that in time would become habitual, almost subconscious.

In an old book of his grandfather's, a book of sailing directions dated 1768, a young cabin boy of an earlier age had written:

> Jeremy Curtis, his hand and pen
> God bless King George and all his men.

Then, underneath, in a different ink:

> Jrm Curtis
> Ag. 8
> 1792.

The son, the nephew, the grandson of some world-travelling captain had inscribed the book back in the days of the French revolution. Boys from captains' families often went to sea as young children, sharing the dangers and hardships of men. Too young to be of much use on deck, they were messengers for the captain and the mate; they held lanterns, sharpened pens, stoked fires in the cabin, fetched sextants to the quarter deck or food from the galley. After ten years of being servants to the officers, picking up the elements of seamanship and navigation, and making one or two voyages as able seamen, they might graduate to a second mate. An illiterate deck hand could never get past bo'sun. He was from another class, and wouldn't start sailing until he was big enough to become an apprentice seaman — fourteen perhaps.

Those days were over, and yet Jonathan, at the age of twelve, was sailing in his grandfather's ship, "signed on" as a cabin boy in an era when cabin boys scarcely existed any longer, half working boy, half passenger, privileged in a way that young deck hands were not.

A captain can rarely sit on deck with a boy teaching him the knots, but a mate or a bo'sun can do it, or if they are too busy, then any of the sailors during their "watch below." Jonathan remembered vividly the young bo'sun who had taught him the more difficult knots. He can see himself sitting on the broad drum of the capstan near the forepeak, fingers busy with the mysteries of the bowline.

"That's it," the young sailor says, hovering beside him. "You can do it if you think hard about it, right?"

"Unhunh ..." he looks into the sea-blue eyes of his friend and teacher, his first grown-up friend who is not a member of his family. He smiles broadly at the sailor. "What's next?"

"Next? You just keep doing it until your fingers can do it by themselves, without being told — till you can do it with your eyes shut." The man rumples Jonathan's hair, which hasn't been cut lately. They're silent for a few minutes while Jonathan ties and unties a dozen bowlines, slowly at first, then more and more quickly.

"How's that? I'm doing it OK?"

"Good, but not quite fast enough yet. And when you've mastered that one, there's the *running* bowline."

"How do you make it?"

"I'll show you as soon as you can do the bowline with one hand, or both hands behind your back. Take your pick." He laughs. From where Jonathan sits his eyes are level with the sailor's; he smiles happily, looking down at the cord in his hands. He tries to make the knot behind his back, gets hopelessly tangled, then laughs and drops the line across his legs. His eyes search the sailor's face. In the sailor's eyes he can see his own reflection looking back. If he could see small enough, would there be a tiny reflection of the sailor in the eyes of the reflected boy? (And so on and on, of course.) He smiles broadly at the thought. The man picks up the line and passes it back to him.

"You're a darling boy. I wish you were my kid brother. I really do. But you've got to learn to stick with things, to keep at them till you master them completely."

Jonathan regards his friend soberly, then he ties ten more bowlines, obediently. Next he tries it one-handed. It is difficult, but by now he knows the turns and twists of the knot so well that he can just manage it, pushing the loose end through the small loop with his thumb, and twisting it around the standing part. He looks up in triumph. "There! I've done it, right?'

"Right. I told you. It's just practice."

Jonathan slides off the capstan, stands close to the sailor, his head level with the man's chin. "I'm sure lucky to find a friend like you on this ship. I sure am."

"Let's say we're both lucky. Now, if you'll sit here on the deck and pay close attention, I'll show you the running bowline. You can make a loop with it, any size you want, and it'll tighten when you toss it over something, but it'll never jam — a bit like the hangman's knot that you most likely tied as a kid, but ... much neater ... see?"

"Say, I really like that one. You could make a lasso."

"I guess you could, only we're not wrangling calves, or whatever it is you do with lassos. But you might toss it over a wharf gump, or use it to fish a spar out of the water."

"Or catch a whale ..."

"Come on, now!" Cy pauses, reflecting. "I just remembered, though ... You've heard of Captain Bob Bartlett?"

"Sure. He went to the North Pole."

"Well ... almost. He lassoed a polar bear one time."

"He did!"

"Yes. From a boat. The bear was in the water. Bartlett hoisted it on board his ship, took it to New York, and sold it to a zoo."

"OK. Show me once again, right slow. Then I'll try it."

They are silent while he memorizes the turns of the knot.

"You sure catch on fast."

"I ... I don't think I'm so smart. You just make it easy ... and ... and I try hard because I want to please you."

The man puts his arm around the boy. "You're great," he says, "and you'll make a first-class sailor. Meanwhile, you've got something to show the captain tomorrow ... And me, too — I've got *you* to show off, what a clever teacher I am!"

"Will the mate let me join your watch?"

"Sure, if I ask him. You think you're big enough to work on deck?"

"Well ... I could *help*."

Then, during the passage home, there was the long run down the Northeast Trades to the Caribbean, men lounging about the decks day after day with little to do, the mate fretting a little about their idleness, watching them play mouth organs and spin yarns — but Joshua was not one of those captains who feels sailors must be kept busy every minute of their watch on deck. There might be emergencies on the way north when they'd have to work around the clock; right now they could relax and conserve their energies.

After that there were those wonderful islands, so blessed by every gift that nature can bestow, so cursed by human greed and ruthlessness. Jonathan always felt, after he grew up, that everyone ought to see the Caribbean islands at least once, not as a tourist, but as a visitor, able to mingle in the life of the little ports and the inland villages.

It was quite different from anything he had experienced at home, but with some resemblances to the Newfoundland outports. He saw black men working big seines for fish along the shore, not dressed in oilskins as they would be at home, but in mere scraps of clothing, not working from boats, as the men of Cupids and Hibbs's Hole would do, but wading up to their chests in the sea, sometimes even swimming when out of their depth. It was a more intimate connection between fish and fishermen than anything he had imagined. They dried up the seines by drawing them up on the beach, and there were the flipping fish, small but plentiful, looking like things plated in nickel.

Other men were building shallops and small ships on cradles beside the sea, two-masted sailers for inter-island trade, or single-masted, open sloops that they sailed with great skill and daring in the roughest waters. Everything seemed to be made at home — ships, houses, food, clothing — it all came from land or sea by the work of human hands.

He saw women taking produce to the markets, loads of fruit and vegetables in huge baskets balanced effortlessly on their heads. He saw potters in hill villages working in open sheds, children taking baths at village pumps, little donkeys carrying huge loads of palm thatch for somebody's roof or strings of pots to the open-air market beside the harbour. He heard palm trees rustling continuously in the trade wind. He marvelled at the sudden fall of night when the sun went down. He walked through a banana plantation, admiring the giant tree-like plants that would bear fruit just once, and then die.

But it was none of this that he would treasure for a lifetime. That memory, that nostalgia, was reserved for the passage itself, the life of the ship in the sea that he learned to love and to yearn for in later years. Even more than his friendship with Cy, even more than his worship of Captain Joshua, it was the ship and the sea that had taken possession of his heart.

Sarah's hand ran through Jonathan's hair, gently. For a moment he was still on deck, twelve years old, with the bo'sun who had befriended him.

"Cy would be disappointed with me," Jonathan told her, "and Grandfather too. They wanted me to be a sailor. They gave me whatever they had to give, and told me I had the makings of a really first-class salt water man. And I believed them. But I allowed Father to send me off to university and turn me into a professor."

"Surely that's not so bad is it, Jonathan? We've had a good life, and we've been a useful part of society, opening the minds of young people, teaching them to appreciate the monuments of unaging intellect."

Jonathan suspected she was being ironic. He laughed bitterly. "Is that how you see it? I see it as a waste of time — my time and theirs."

"Even if just *one* student takes fire because of you..."

"Oh, cut it out, Sarah! That one student goes on to publish papers on 'The Rise of Realism in French Fiction of the Nineteenth Century,' right?"

She laughed, and kissed him. "We'll go sailing together before the autumn semester gets us boxed in. It won't be the same as racing for the Yucatan Channel with the wind on the quarter and foam flying from the bow, but we can taste salt spray for a few days, and you can teach Judith to tie bowlines and things."

He brightened, and joined in her laughter. "At least with your old professor you won't have to go pacing around one of those 'widow's walks' on the roof of a house, gazing endlessly out to sea."

The Wall

The young hitch-hiker, like a thousand others, was travelling through Canada with whoever would give him a lift. Maybe nineteen years old, he was slightly bearded, hair longish, clothes quite haphazard — from Frenchie's Good Used Clothing, most likely — clean, but worn. The boy too was clean, and lean, almost painfully thin, in fact — rather a contrast to himself, Jonathan reflected, *Doctor Johnnie*, heavy-set, and a bit set in his ways, if the truth must be admitted. Back in his home-town in Newfoundland they might have referred to him as "burned down in the fat," a phrase from sealing days when ships got into a large patch of seals, and allowed their fires to go down while they loaded up with pelts. Jonathan and Sarah — double-income Canadians, with "good jobs" and virtually no purpose at all in life, had allowed their fires to go down a bit — not all the way, he hoped.

"How far are you going, me son?"

"All the way." The young man laughed. "Vancouver, if I can make it that far."

"Well, I'm not heading across Canada myself, but I can take you as far as Moncton if you want to hitch up the wild and wooly coastal route, or on to Saint John, if you prefer the more civilised road along the Saint John River."

"Saint John would be just fine, I guess — a pretty good ride for the first day. You heading for the States?"

"Well, *through* the States to Ontario. I drive back and forth to Halifax two or three times a year, visiting lecturer at a college there, but my regular job is in Guelph, where my wife and I both teach English. My name's Jonathan Kirby."

"I thought you might be a professor. You look like it. I'm Johnny LeValliant, and I'm afraid I don't do anything much. Last job I had was in Sydney, pushing hamburgers."

"LeValliant! Haven't met the name since I left Newfoundland. Channel Islands, isn't it?"

"Maybe. I don't know."

"I'm pretty sure it is. A family with that name used to live next door to me when I was about the age you are now. There were two little kids, a girl about four, and a seven-year-old boy named Kenny."

"Why, that must have been my uncle Ken! You're from St. John's?"

"Almost. Brigus."

"That's it. That's where they lived for a while, before they moved to St. John's. I think their father might have been a cable operator there."

"Yes, my father was too, but he was a native of Brigus — a beautiful old town, full of retired ships' captains in those days — my own grandfather was one of them. Everything there seemed ancient — even the white picket fences, and the two-storey and three-storey wooden houses. Old shade trees and old-fashioned flowers. We had a garden with a brick wall that looked like it might have been built by John Guy's colonists."

"So you knew my Uncle Ken! He died last year, out in Calgary. And that little girl would be my Aunt Marian. She's still living. Never married or had kids, or anything like that."

"You from Halifax?"

"Sort of. I was at Dal for a year. Couldn't hack it."

"You want to talk?"

"Sure. Tell me about Brigus. I've never been there."

That garden wall, Jonathan reflected, had actually been built some time before the First World War, perhaps in those years when ice captains from Brigus were trying to get American explorers to the North Pole. In those times tradesmen worked for a few cents an hour, and a master mariner could build practically anything that took his fancy out of the pay from a foreign voyage or two. The wall was six and a half feet high, dark red brick, softened by time, with patches of moss and lichens, and clumps of tiny ferns wherever the old trees cast enough shade for them. Between his garden and the one next door the wall faced southwest, and was warmed with sun heat, especially in spring and autumn — a great place to sit and read, or work on a school assignment.

His grandfather had probably laid much of the brick himself, working between voyages with the help of a hired mason. He had put in a bench of driftwood, wharf planks, probably, two feet wide and four inches thick, where Jonathan liked to sit on warm afternoons. He had a vague memory of sitting there with his grandfather while he was still very young, listening to tales of the sea, before his grandfather had abandoned the house to his son's family, and moved down toward the waterfront. A chickadee had lit on the edge of the wall just above his head, leaning forward, announcing its presence with a monotonous chant. Perhaps the chickadee had wanted him to move so it could pick clusters of hatching spider's eggs out of the moss.

"Kenny used to climb over the wall to play with me," he told the boy. "The little girl was too young for that, but sometimes she'd come around through the gate. There was so little traffic even young kids could walk around on the roads."

"They weren't afraid of strangers?"

Jonathan was jolted briefly out of time and place. This, he had to remind himself, was Canada, where strangers might just possibly be dangerous. "No stranger where we lived would ever harm a child," he said. "If kids needed to be afraid of anyone, it was people in their own homes."

It must be a spring day that he is remembering, a day with chickadees and hatching spiders, and a small boy coming home from school. It is lovely late May weather. Our memories always seem to be of weather like that. He is working on a highschool assignment. A bit later the light of his life, Virginia, will arrive, and they'll work together. Perhaps it is Parent's Day or something, the senior school closed for the afternoon.

He remembers hearing a door open and close in the adjoining garden. Then a pause of about two minutes, while Kenny sheds his school clothes, and pulls on an old pair of jeans. Next the click of a door closing again. Kenny would now be tiptoeing through the garden barefoot, silent as a cat stalking a mouse. Jonathan pretends not to hear the soft rustle as the boy climbs the wall and perches on top.

Dead silence for a minute. Then a light tickling at Jonathan's right ear. Then his left. He pretends to brush away a spider, or whatever it is, and pretends to be surprised when instead of a spider he encounters a handful of wiggling toes. The boy's laughter comes falling down to him, and then Kenny comes sliding down beside him, asking, at the same time, "Can we go feed the fish?"

"I loved your Uncle Ken when he was a little boy, and I was about fifteen."

"You didn't mind being bothered by a little kid?"

"Oh no, not at all. There was a girl in my class, my 'steady' as we used to say, and I had a best friend who'd grown up with me, a neighbour, but except for my grandfather I was never very close to my family. I had no brothers or sisters. A little boy who treated me like his grown-up brother helped to make up for that. He was lonely, too, in a way. His father was hard on him — hard on both those little kids. Kenny said to me once, 'We'll get a whipping if we go home late,' and the little girl said, 'Daddy has a whip lash,' and Kenny explained, 'She means a buggy whip.'"

"Wow! Didn't you report him or anything?"

"I would now, of course. But in those days you didn't. Every man's house was his castle. Every family had a wall around it, and what happened inside the wall was nobody's business. If a man didn't murder his kids, or maim them, or break his wife's bones, nobody interfered."

"Things have sure changed, haven't they?"

"Yes, just recently. Some ways they're much better, some ways much worse. We're more responsible toward our neighbours nowadays. We feel that society as a whole has a right to protect children, and women to some extent, too. And we know that we can destroy the world by allowing the corporations to exploit it however they like. But mostly we don't do a damn thing about it."

How strange, Jonathan thought, to meet those echoes out of a past that he'd all but forgotten. The LeValliant children hadn't grown up next door to him. The family had moved away within a few months. Kenny as "kid brother" had been replaced by another boy from his school, and he'd heard nothing more from that family for the better part of a lifteime.

"There were no other children in that family were there?" he asked the young man. "How come you call Ken your uncle?"

"No. There were just the two of them. I guess Uncle Ken was actually my dad's first cousin. I got on OK with my own folks — nothing like what you've been talking about."

"I see. So what happened to your Uncle Ken?"

"He married young, I heard, but his marriage didn't last. They said he ran out on the woman."

"Common enough. Faults on both sides, usually. Nothing to hold them together."

"Most likely." The boy was silent for a minute. Then he spoke again: "You said you loved him."

"Yes. But the time was too short, you see — too short for me to do Kenny any real good. It was only a few months, and then they were gone. If you're going to help a child over the hard early years of his life, you've got to love him for years together, like my grandfather did with me."

"You have children of your own, sir?"

"Oh yes. Almost grown up by now. A young woman, living her life in her own way. We've never tried to push her into anything."

It was upsetting, thinking of those two other little kids, in another time, in a place where the streets were safe, walled into the waste land of their own home. And how many others, then — even today — lived behind such walls? Thousands, surely. Millions, perhaps.

And now, Jonathan thought, one was a young-middle-aged woman, and one was dead. Back there, briefly, in a time he'd forgotten, love had flowered between those two small children and a youth just edging toward manhood. And it had come to nothing. The boy was dead. And where was the little girl? Not, surely, imprisoned in that spinster with the dyed perm, Aunt Marian, who was still living, but had never had kids, or anything like that.

Unto the Third and Fourth Generation

At first the baby seemed almost too fragile to touch — a head that appeared to be unduly heavy for the neck (Could its weight, unsupported, damage those delicate vertebrae?) legs that looked as if they might bend like green twigs. Jonathan had limited experience with babies — there'd been just the one, many years ago. He handled this grandchild with the utmost caution. But babies are tougher and stronger than they look, and this baby was soon taking his own weight on legs that were nothing at all like green twigs. Still too top-heavy to stand alone, he would stand on Jonathan's thighs, kept upright by holding hands, and actually dance, rhythmically, both feet together, while Jonathan sang a lively nonsense rhyme.

One day — it seemed only weeks later — there he was, two years old and a bit, running about in a skimpy little shirt, pulling himself up over Jonathan's knees, hoping to be petted or tickled or just hugged, for babies, Jonathan had discovered, have sensual needs — greater sensual needs than older children, many of whom withdraw, gradually, into a private world. The little child snuggled against him, a real person by now, no longer quite a baby, loving it when Jonathan caressed him and tickled his feet and hugged him (not too hard) kissing him under his chin or on the back of his neck.

"The Terrible Twos!" Jonathan thought. "How easy it is to keep this one quiet."

While this was going on Jonathan sipped a glass of rum and cola, and went on talking with his daughter Judith, the child's mother, who had turned out, like his wife Sarah, to be addicted to dialogue. The child never got tired of being petted, and was thoroughly used to adult talk going on over his head. He'd stay in Jonathan's arms for an hour while conversations between older people swirled around him, a babbling brook of sound, or until Jonathan himself decided it was time for something more intellectual than nuzzling.

Reading. Amazing how he'd stay quiet and listen to almost anything. He seemed to enjoy stories that must be far beyond the understanding of a two-year-old. Alice in Wonderland at two and a half, Robinson Crusoe at three. Jonathan taught him some pre-reading skills — the names of the letters, a few simple words, how to put together C-A-T with blocks, how to make CAT SAT ON A MAT with word blocks. But he didn't begin reading for himself until a couple of years later, and then it was baby books with four-word sentences of single syllables. The child was no infant prodigy, thank God.

Or he'd sit on his grandfather's shoulders, hands locked under Jonathan's chin, while they played horse:

> This is the way the farmers ride:
> Hobbledy-hoi, hobbledy-hoi.

This is the way the ladies ride:
Clippity-clop, clippity-clop.
And this is the way the gentlemen ride:
Gallopy-trot! gallopy-trot!

bouncing violently up and down as Jonathan leaped about, the boy crowing with delight.

Another day — arms extended, Jonathan swinging him in a circle by his hands in the water at the edge of a lake, feet kicking up foam, the little boy almost scared, but at the same time thrilled with this new kind of adventure. Or leaping out into space with him among sand dunes — something like the thrill of a suicide jump without the fatal ending. As soon as he was big enough he'd do this alone, while Judith watched, heart in her mouth.

"It *is* possible to get hurt among sand dunes, you know — I've even heard of a child who somersaulted and broke his neck."

"Not *this* child, Judith. He isn't suicidal or accident-prone. Let's not teach him to be over-cautious. We're not raising him for the civil service."

And afterwards, in a hot tub, he'd be all soap and bubbles, and as slippery as a fish in Jonathan's arms, and there'd be a fine mess of splashes and puddles that they'd have to clean up together. There weren't many rules with Judith; one of the few of them was, Whoever makes a mess cleans it up.

"So this is being a grandparent," he said. "It sure makes growing old worthwhile!"

"Wait till I call on you for the money to send him to college," she laughed.

"We'll manage, I'm sure. I'll start an education fund tomorrow. After all, he's my only grandchild."

"So far," she said.

"And besides, he may not want to go to college, even if *you* think he should. He's not going to be *sent* anywhere he doesn't want to go — there's far too much of that. Maybe he'll want to be a seaman like his great-grandfather, and all his earlier ancestors. There's still a big traffic in the great waters, even if we don't notice it, here in landlocked Ontario."

"He'd still have to go to navigation school, or wherever it is you have to go to learn those things."

"Yes, I suppose he would, nowadays. This continent is in love with classrooms. We still haven't returned to apprenticeship, which is the best of all learning systems."

"There's some of it — in business college at least," she said. "Students go out for a semester to work on computers and things."

"Good idea, so far as it goes, and 'twould be a lot better for science students if they spent more time as assistants to the great masters, and less plodding through textbooks and nodding through lectures."

"What do you know about science courses, anyway?"

"Not much," he admitted. "Meanwhile, how about I take this boy to the park to feed the ducks?"

"Yes. Leave me to my correspondence course."

"Oh? You haven't told me about it."

"I will later, if it seems to be working out. And ... I should tell you... I love the way you play with that little kid. He has the most wonderful time with you. 'Twould be hard for any father to do as well. Did you play with me like that?"

"Certainly. Don't you remember?"

"Not really, just some vague impressions, so much has happened since. Could I have repressed it because it was so sensual?"

"Judith! Don't be ridiculous."

"And I don't remember ever hearing you say you loved me — ever, in all my life."

"Well, don't you know that I do?"

"Of course."

"There you are. It's only when you don't love someone that you have to keep telling them that you do. Real love never needs to be put into words; it expresses itself in a multitude of ways."

"Yes. I remember how Duncan kept calling me 'sweetheart' and saying he loved me, while he didn't really love anyone except himself, of course. He just wanted sex without having to work for it. You and Sarah are the really permanent things in my life, you know. You're always there, always loving me, always reliable, never changing."

"You make us sound like the Rock of Ages."

"Well — all my other relationships have been so transient. Tell me, how have you and Mother managed to stay together all those years?"

"By not working at it, that's how. Once you begin *working* at a marriage, it generally can't be salvaged. With us, there was no problem. We fell in love the day we met. Love, not lust, was how it began, nurturing each other's souls, not grasping at each other's bodies. We'd had all that before. Soon our lives were entangled beyond all separation, and we're still in love, a quarter of a century later."

"It's not that way with most people. Some of the strongest unions among my small circle of friends are of people who separated, and then came back together. I guess

I loved Duncan for a while, but there'll be no reunion, and now that he and I are going separate ways, and he's agreed to let me have little Joshua without strings or conditions, and put it all down in writing, signed and notarized, I have to think about what I'm going to do with the rest of my life."

"You can go back to living with me and Sarah for a start, and raising this kid, and helping keep the roses in shape."

"Yes. For a start. But I have to think about what I want to do: not earning a living, I mean. There's always welfare. People tell me you can get along on welfare if you don't live in a big city or an expensive suburb. I'd make out as a welfare mother. But the fact is, I want to do something more than make out."

"From your tone, I'd bet that you already know what you want to do. You've already decided."

"Yes, Jonathan, I have. I want to be a writer."

"Oh God! Oh sweet suffering Jesus!"

"My dear father! Are you ill?"

"No Judith. Just shocked. Millions of people want to be writers. One out of every ten thousand manages it. If you're not talking about journalism — and I assume you're not — then you've chosen the world's most difficult, most demanding profession. Did you know that?"

"More or less, yes. I had a pretty good idea that it wouldn't be easy."

"Let me tell you about my own experience with writers. I've known a dozen or more who were successful enough to be invited to residencies at universities where I was teaching. They were all wonderful people in various ways, mostly hard drinkers, using alcohol to help them cope with their difficult lives, modest about their careers, and friendly with bumpkins like myself who had not a glimmer of their genius. They were all surrounded with mobs of eager students who were all writing like mad, all seemingly well supplied with talent, all going to win the Nobel Prize for literature ten years from now. And out of all those hundreds and hundreds of young people, some of them showing every indication that they were born to be writers, exactly two that I know of got far enough to be short-listed for a Governor General's Award, but not even those two managed to make a career out of it."

"So maybe I'll wind up as an editor."

"Now there you're beginning to make sense. Editors, if they're good enough, sometimes graduate into writers. Even journalists sometimes do — one out of a hundred who try it. Hemingway was a journalist in Canada before he became a writer."

"You don't have much confidence in me, it seems."

"I want you to be happy, Judith. I don't care a tinker's damn whether or not you achieve what people call success. Success isn't necessarily harmful, but it often makes people unhappy. First you have to have talent. Then you have to have the ambition to use it, the character to survive disappointment, and to keep going, for years if necessary, while no one believes in you, and, if you are successful, then you need still more character to survive the stresses and demands that success imposes. To escape all those pitfalls, you really need to be one of what St. Matthew called 'the very elect.'"

She came and kissed him lightly. "Run on and feed the ducks," she said.

He took little Joshua by the hand and went prowling about the kitchenette. "There'll be more creatures than ducks to feed," he told Joshua. "Let's forage around for surplus comestibles."

They took an apple, sliced into chunks, and found a pancake left from breakfast generously smeared with maple syrup.

"Just what we need," he said. "We'll be as popular as pink lemonade in August. Come on Jay. You can carry the loot."

After they'd thrown a few dozen scraps of dry bread to the ducks, and coaxed them up the bank to their feet, they walked off through the park hand in hand, the little boy carrying the plastic bag of food.

The racoons heard them walking, and peered down out of the trees where they were having their siesta. They soon spotted the food bag, and came walking down the trunks head-first, turning their heads to peer at the visitors. When they were all the way down, Jonathan let Joshua hold out a piece of apple. A racoon took it, not in his teeth as most animals would do, but very gently in his two front paws. Then another did the same, and so on.

"See how careful they are not to hurt or frighten you."

"Yes. Pretty."

"You can touch their fur if you like, but just touch. They don't want to be petted, like a cat or a dog."

"Pretty pets."

"Yes, but they don't make very good pets. They're too smart, and too wilful, too clever with their paws. They can open closets and drawers and take the caps off jars, and make a mess of everything in your house. You'll hardly believe this, but many Americans used to kill them, just to use their tails and skin for fur hats. They still do it in what they call The South."

"Bad," the child said.

"Bad people, yes, but they didn't know any better — still don't in some places."

They walked on, and found the bear, a full-grown animal standing on hind legs and working his way around a spacious wire enclosure. He didn't need to see what they had in the bag. He could smell it. He poked his nose through the wire and whined like a puppy, so they fed him bits of syrupy pancake, and he got down on his back and waved his paws, begging for more. The little boy laughed.

"Big," he said. "Big dog."

"Not a dog, but I see what you mean. He certainly acts like one, doesn't he?"

The bear was as carefully gentle as the racoons. He licked their fingers, seeking the last smidgeon of maple syrup. Then another visitor, a teenage boy, came by with a bottle of Pepsi half empty. He passed the bottle to the bear, and the bear took it into the cage, held it in both paws, and tipped it up to his open mouth, just like a child.

"I wouldn't do that, son, if I were you," Jonathan said.

"Why not, sir?"

"Well, bears will eat anything sweet. Wild ones go looking for honey trees, and tear out the honey combs to eat, even when they get stung by the bees. But I don't think soft drinks are exactly good for them."

"I'll only give him a sip, next time."

"Yes. That would be OK, I guess."

"Is this your little boy?"

"My grandson, yes."

"Does he go on the swings?"

"Yes, he loves it."

"I could push him for you. He's too small to work the swing by himself."

"Sure. We'll take turns. Would you like to ride him on your shoulders?"

First lesson in human brotherhood, Jonathan thought. Most of the people you meet want to be friends, and not one in a thousand is even the slightest bit dangerous. They pushed little Joshua way up into the sky, and the boy took him down the corkscrew turns of the plastic slide in his arms, and gave him back to Jonathan and said, "Some day I'll have a kid like that."

"And the kid will be one of the lucky ones," Jonathan thought.

When they returned to the apartment Sarah and Judith were both there, Sarah having finished her morning with a class of freshmen — or mostly, in fact, freshwomen, since few males, nowadays, bothered with the so-called humanities.

"What a pity you haven't made it to pension age," Sarah greeted her husband. "You're a perfect baby sitter. Judy could go out to work without having to put the child into day care."

"I'm not putting him into day care in any case," Judith said. "I'm all for day care as a general principle, for people who need it, but it would be a last resort, so far as I'm concerned."

"Chip off the old block," Sarah said. "When you were small we took you everywhere, even where children weren't supposed to be welcome. Jonathan used to say we didn't need to go any place that practised age segregation."

"Separating kids into age classes and calling them 'peer groups' was never in much favour with us," Jonathan said. "Maybe I was influenced by memories of outport life, where children blend into every group, and tend to relate most strongly to older children, who may not always like them very much, but who always tolerate them, and feel responsible for their safety."

"Yes, I remember those visits to Brigus," Judith said. "There were always cousins and aunts' young sisters and so on, willing to play with us and to take us along on their expeditions. The boys even let me go trouting with them. Where else would you find boys who'd take a five-year-old girl trouting?"

"Lots of places," Jonathan said, "but very few of them in North America, more's the pity. You know, I think perhaps the greatest thing the outports had to teach us was human solidarity."

"Oh, that was just one thing," Sarah said. "I learned thousands of things from the outport women, from women who'd almost forgotten how to read after they dropped out of school in grade eight. They were natural feminists, for one thing. I don't mean they were jealous of men, or anything like that. They accepted the need for sex roles. But they had a solid sense of their own worth, and of a common cause with members of their own sex. You could call the women of any outport a sisterhood or a sorority, a more effective one than those in the colleges, and you wouldn't be far wrong."

"And, of course, they had all the traditional skills that had been passed along for generations," Jonathan said. "They taught that, too: how to gut a fish, how to cope with a broody hen, how to stop nosebleeds, or deliver babies, if necessary."

"All that and more," Sarah said. "I wonder if it still survives."

"It's passing, unfortunately. There has been an overpowering tide of subtle propaganda teaching the people of the outports that the mainland way is the only right way, that electric stoves are superior to wood fires, and that microwaves are superior to both."

"It will come back," Judith said, "just as people (real people, not plastics) went back to baking their own bread, mixing muffins from fruits and cereals, putting up pickles and preserves. It will all come back." She paused, reflecting. "And children will be loved again the way Jonathan loves them — not by being shut up behind bars in a playpen with a lot of expensive and boring toys, but by being held in human arms and soothed with human speech, and reassured that they are not objects, but real people, worthy of being loved."

"Bravo!" said Jonathan. "Just for that I'll take you all out to dinner. How about the Stone Crock up in St. Jacob's? Mennonite food. Real country cooking. A great place for big appetites and little kids."

Music at the Close

Death may come like a stroke of lightning, or it may sneak up on you without warning, or in many other ways. "Behold I come as a thief," said the angel of the Apocalypse. Azriel — was that his name? — the angel of the darker drink, as Fitzgerald called him, hovered for a long time barely at the edge of Jonathan's consciousness, then, more and more became a presence that he and Sarah could not ignore.

In their forty-five years together (nearly half a century! he reflected) she had been so healthy, so completely without the need of doctors, that she at first dismissed what she believed might be a temporary indisposition. It seemed such a slight thing — a lack of energy, an occasional sense of confusion, a tendency to tire easily, intolerance for certain foods that she had formerly enjoyed — that it could be ignored, but gradually it all began to coalesce into a pattern of weakness and decline. By that time the diagnosis was clear and the visits to the doctor had multiplied, but the outlook was still uncertain: a forty to fifty percent chance that chemotherapy might work the way it is supposed to, otherwise, temporary improvements, but not permanent recovery.

A few weeks later it was obvious that the treatments were providing only intermittent regressions; then she and Jonathan and their daughter Judith gradually came to accept the inevitable, and the specialist was talking in terms of months rather than years.

"Sometimes these things go quickly," he told her. "Sometimes there are long periods when you can continue to work at a reduced pace; you may even feel better for a while; once in every thousand cases or so there is even a spontaneous recovery. That's what happens at Lourdes and such places often enough to confirm a belief in faith healing, but temporary remissions are much more likely. Try to live normally. That way you'll likely escape the misery of a long terminal illness, and of course we can provide palliative treatment with drugs." (At least, she reflected, he didn't call the drugs "medication.")

Jonathan seemed to be more devastated by all this than Sarah herself. He became haggard, lost weight, lost sleep, found his work at the university almost intolerable, and warned his department that he might have to apply for leave.

Judith was more philosophical. "There'll be time to adjust," she said, "time to tie up any loose ends between us, time to get used to the idea of her death."

"That doesn't change the emptiness that lies ahead," Jonathan told her.

"No, but we can at least make some plans to cope with it before it's actually on top of us. This won't be the kind of horror you'd face if you were called out of a lecture hall one day and told she'd been killed on the street."

"Oh Lord!" He paused, reflecting. "I'm not sure that a sudden shock would be any harder to bear. I'll try to work to the end of the semester, but I've already warned them that I'll have to have leave of absence if she gets critically ill before then. A lifetime of interdependence is hard to shake, you know, and I'm going to spend every possible minute with her."

For Jonathan that was when the dreams began. In one of the first that he remembered after waking, he was back with his grandfather, Captain Joshua, in a boat near the headland between Brigus and Cupids in Newfoundland's Conception Bay, jigging for codfish. He recognizes the sudden, familiar weight on the line, and draws the fish steadily toward the surface, taking in the line hand over hand, letting it fall on the floorboards between his feet. He can look down through the water and see the green-black shape of the big fish moving beneath the surface. Then, suddenly, the line is slack, and the fish disappears, diving into deep water.

Try again. Toss the jigger a couple of yards out from the gun'all, wait for it to sink, then move it in short tugs a few feet above the bottom. There is a bump, but it is a false alarm, a jerk on the line that seems somehow unlike a fish, afterwards nothing at all, not even the weight of the leaden fish-shaped jigger. The line is clean and empty. Try another jigger. But there isn't one. Somehow the tackle box has become empty. There is nothing in it — nothing at all. He wonders about cod hooks. Yes, sure enough, there are cod hooks that have appeared from somewhere, and a strip of sheet lead with which he can wrap them together to make a jigger of sorts. But try as he will the wrapping never comes out right. He can't make the hooks stay in place.

And then, in one of those scene shifts where dreams ape the movies, he is no longer in the boat, but on a wharf with a crowd of strangers, and his grandfather is no longer there. At that point he knows he is dreaming, and wakes with a feeling of emptiness and frustration.

He is back in college, but not in the one he knew as an undergraduate. It is a strange place with endless corridors and unmarked doors. He has to write an exam today, an exam in mathematics, his most demanding subject. He is on his way to a room where the papers will be passed out, but he can't remember which exam he is supposed to write. Is it elementary calculus, theory of invariants, symbolic logic? Surely he passed the first one years ago, and has never dabbled in the others. Somehow, the number 666 is mixed up with it. Is that the number of the room he is supposed to find? If only he could remember, he could ask one of the passing students for directions ...

This time he is a university lecturer. He knows he is going to be late for class, has a minute or two at most, and has lost his lecture notes. They must be on his desk ... in a drawer ... in his briefcase ... perhaps on a shelf beside the books ... The longer he looks, the more places seem to be possible ... under the desk, on the floor ... in the waste paper basket ... that's it! those crumpled and torn papers, just scraps, even smaller than when he first looked at them. Can he possibly fit them together, patch them with mending tape? The more paper he fishes out of the basket, the more there appears to be ...

He has to make an emergency phone call. There has been an accident, and he has been asked to call an ambulance. It is only a three-digit number, but he gets the digits all mixed up, starts with the wrong one, tries again, gets a recording that gives him meaningless instructions, hangs up, tries again; meanwhile the phone has turned into one of those ancient wall-mounted models with a handle you have to crank. How many cranks? He has no idea. He has never used anything like this before ...

Jonathan, unused to analysing, or even remembering, his own dreams, does not connect his nightly frustration with his inability to do anything to halt Sarah's progress toward death. He does not blame himself consciously. He knows that in such matters you should rely on whatever the art of medicine has achieved, up to now. In some areas the achievements have been great, indeed; in the matter of chronic, fatal illness, the achievements have been pitifully small.

Sarah's condition grew worse only slowly, but steadily. She quit working and spent her time at home, at first seated at her desk, reading and writing, then more and more hours of each day in bed, often asleep, sometimes in a quiet, trance-like state that she seemed to be able to maintain contentedly for long stretches. While Sarah could still help herself, Judith got leave of absence from her editing job, and came to stay with her mother

"I know you don't really need me," she said. "It's *I* who need *you*. We have to catch up on the conversations we've missed in recent years, when we were both too busy to talk. While you can still manage it, without getting unduly tired, I want to get from you everything that I can."

"Well, whatever I can do," Sarah said. "You can have my accumulated knowledge of English literature, to add to your own wide reading, if it's any good to you. Or my knowledge of how to conduct your life according to the principles of the *Tao-teh-King*." She laughed lightly. "Is that what you're after?"

"I'm after your capacity for love, if the truth must be told. I'm hoping to catch a glimmer of the light that your students see in you. I'm hoping to learn how to love someone for half a century, as you've done with Jonathan."

"My, that's a big order." Sarah paused, considering. "It's a gratuitous grace. All you can really do is pray for it. It can't be learned."

"I was afraid that might be so, but perhaps grace, like evil, is catching. Rub up against it long enough, and a little might rub off on you."

Sarah laughed. "It's a good theory. Anyway, there's no great mystery about life-long attachments, if that's what you're talking about — Jonathan and me? Many animals mate for life. Wolves do. And Canada geese."

"But it's something more than mating."

"Oh yes. Much more."

"A lifelong commitment of the whole person, isn't it?"

"Who are we, Judith, to say that a goose is incapable of such a commitment? Or a wolf? Just because it isn't common among people, at least in our culture, in this century? How do we know what emotional depths exist in other creatures?"

"So all I can do is pray?"

"I didn't mean that literally. Prayer works for some people, for people with a religious gift. But there's none of that in our family that I've ever noticed."

"Anyway, you're doing just fine, Sarah. This is the kind of thing I wanted. I'm not tiring you?"

"I'm still pretty strong, Judith. You'll notice it when I become feeble, and that may be pretty soon — who knows? I'm glad I can still be of some use."

With Jonathan there was much less need for talk. Many years earlier they had reached something like total understanding, but one day he praised her for "being brave."

"I'm not fighting it, Jonathan," she said, "none of this *Reader's Digest* stuff about battling to the bitter end, throwing the burning torch to your family, and so on. None of that, for me. Kicking and screaming against the inevitable might have suited Dylan Thomas. You know, 'Rage, rage against the dying of the light.' I'm not a halfcrazy alcoholic."

"Dying isn't that difficult," she told him on another occasion. "The suffering might be, if there was a lot of it, but the dying isn't. Like birth, it happens of itself." She kept her sense of humour to the end: "Modern medicine," she said, "really comes into its own with the business of dying. Doctors can only rarely help you to live, but they can almost always help you to die."

Jonathan's laughter was forced. He found little joy in those hours he spent with Sarah during her last illness. She understood this, and tried to help him bear it, but with little success. As she grew weaker, she also grew quieter, but continued to share with him her thoughts and feelings, mostly in brief snatches, but now and then in more extended communication:

"Dreams," she said. "I dream all the time. The dreams are vivid and continuous, and mostly very pleasant. Often I'm walking in a tropical garden, in a world that seems more real than waking life. Some part of my mind is becoming more creative, as my body grows weaker. Does that make sense? Each time I wake from one of those long slumbers that have become so common, I have a sinking feeling, as though the real world were fading out, and a bleak fantasy taking its place."

There was little pain, and only bearable discomfort. She didn't ask what drugs were being prescribed, but the sedatives seemed to affect only her body; her mind remained clear, if placid. After a while she could not get out of bed without help. Her skin had become not just pale, but transparent, like the skin of a grape. She had taken on a new kind of beauty, Jonathan realized: she looked not so much frail as spiritual.

"I dreamed we were on a ship," she told him. "You were just as you were when we first met, young and lithe and beautiful, and there were other people on the ship, too, but they all became ill, and disappeared one by one — going below to their bunks, I suppose. Then there was a storm, and you and I had to manage the ship together, just the two of us. And you know, I felt wonderful. I was trying to help you as much as I could, but I was quite sure that you could bring us safe to port. The storm roared, but there was music in the storm, too, and birds of some kind — storm petrels? — I don't know, but they were beautiful, like butterflies, and the music sang through the rigging like the strings of a wind harp — and you were just wonderful, Jonathan — a young god among the elements...." So saying, she fell asleep again.

"This woman loves me now as well as then," he told Judith. "It's easy to go on loving the person you first met, the image of the beautiful teenager, the divine Beatrice — such love can last a lifetime and lead only to poetry, but to go on loving not the image, but the changing reality — that's quite another matter. To go with the flow, to change with a changing love, to continue it life-long is a rare and wonderful experience."

"Sarah says it leads to a maturing and deepening of the spirit," Judith told him.

"*Agape, philia, karitas, eros*," Jonathan murmured. "Most of the saints knew two or three of them but missed the fourth. It is only when you experience the rare combination of all four that you know life in its most beautiful aspect."

"Seeing you and Sarah together at this stage is just wonderful for me," Judith said. "Inspiring. I wonder ... Should I ask my son to quit his job and come here to spend a while with us?"

"For young Joshua it wouldn't be the same," Jonathan said. "He's always loved Sarah, but he's separated from her by two generations. Of course he should see her once more before she dies — just at the end, perhaps — but you couldn't expect him to draw such inspiration from her as you seem to be able to do."

"Um ... perhaps not."

"We haven't discussed any ... arrangements ... afterwards," Jonathan said.

"She talked with me about that," Judith told him. "She didn't want to distress you any more than you already are distressed. Of the two of us, she thinks I'm the stronger, and that you need to be protected."

"She may be right. I certainly don't feel very strong."

"Yes. Anyway, there's to be no funeral or memorial ceremony. She doesn't want any mumbo-jumbo, or any of the usual hypocrisy that happens at the time of death. Her body is to go to the medical school, then to be disposed of in whatever way they dispose of cadivars. We can put a small memorial stone in the cemetary at Brigus, if we wish, simply giving her dates, and stating she was your wife."

"Yes," Jonathan whispered. "Yes, of course. That's the way I'd want it, too. As usual, our minds work together."

And then one day, very close to the end, Sarah said, "I have something for you, Jonathan. You might call it a last gift."

"Every day of your life has been a gift to me, Sarah," he said. But at that point she drifted off to sleep, perhaps failing to hear his reply.

When she awoke, she seemed to have forgotten about it, but a little later she called to him, "Jonathan, I'm sure there's a bottle of good wine, isn't there? Let's have a glass together."

He brought glasses, with his best claret, and pulled up a chair beside her bed.

"Remember that first afternoon in the Humber Valley — the *Rubyiat*, and so on?"

"Of course, I could never forget."

"Well, this is such an occasion. I have a poem for you. That's the gift."

"A poem! But..."

"Yes, I know. I've never written anything in my life, except letters and test papers. But suddenly ... well, some people get religion when they're dying, you know. I seem to have got poetry. Writing things down is too much effort for me, but that doesn't matter. The lines come into my head ready-made during those long trances that are so much like sleep."

Jonathan poured two glasses of the dark red wine, each two-thirds full, and inhaled the boquet from one of them. Sarah took just a sip, and rolled it around her tongue.

"Do you have a pen, Jonathan? I want you to write it down. Later you can give it to the archives, or frame it as a family heirloom. It rhymes. I hope that won't turn you off?"

Jonathan wrote the lines down as she gave them to him, slowly, one at a time:

> I think of those who braved the world's vexation,
> to seek for truth like water on a thorn,
> that brought them peace and bloody consummation,
> glory and shame and scorn.
>
> I fear that we shall never find by searching
> the lofty ecstasies of those who trod
> the stations of so many crosses, lurching
> up the steep stairs of God:
>
> eternal children in a land of wonder,
> playing with lily-cup and golden-rod,
> eternal pilgrims bowing lowly under
> the sky-blue hands of God.
>
> Cold are our days, and marble-cold the chancel
> where the dead Christ lies on his gilded bier —
> and reason has maternal power to cancel
> each hope, or dream, or prayer.

She lay still, with closed eyes, apparently exhausted by the effort. Then she whispered: "Is it any good?"

"It's beautiful," Jonathan assured her. "And very bleak — which means that it's appropriate — and very true with respect to our time. I never would have guessed you could do that sort of thing, Sarah."

"Me either ... Pass me the glass, Jonathan."

"Yes. A toast. To music at the close?"

"To music." They drained the wine, and Sarah passed at once into a deep sleep, right in the middle of a sentence: "One glass is ..."

A few days later Joshua arrived, a tall, dark young man, looking very clean and sailor-like. If he was shocked by Sarah's frailty he didn't show it. He kissed her as someone might kiss a flower, and sat beside her talking of his travels, as long as she remained awake.

"When I have children I'll give them copies of your poetry," he said, "and all their lives they'll be able to refer to 'my great-grandmother, the poet.' How do you do it?"

"I don't really do anything, Joshua. It just comes to me, a line or two at a time, and in a few days the poem is complete. I go over it in my mind and memorise it as it comes to me. I have another shaping itself now, a line at a time. I don't know if it will ever be complete, of course."

"You'll finish it," he said.

"I suppose so. Maybe the discovery of this strange gift is keeping me alive beyond my time. And now ... if you don't mind ... I have to sleep a lot, you know."

"Yes. Pleasant dreams, Sarah."

Later he told her of his progress as a seaman: "I'll have my ticket in navigation by the end of the year. Then I'll be able to qualify as second mate on a seagoing ship, perhaps sail to Europe and the West Indies."

"I'm glad you're following the family tradition, Joshua. You'll be a captain, like your great-grandfather, the man you are named for."

"Actually he'd be my great-great-grandfather, wouldn't he?"

"Oh yes, that's right. He was my grandfather-in-law."

"I'm only sorry he isn't alive, he could have told me so much about the sea."

"Yes," said Jonathan, "and I wish he could have seen you doing this. It would have pleased him so much to see you following the sea, the way he expected me to do, and aiming to be a master mariner like himself."

"I just can't wait to be in charge of a ship. I want it more than anything."

"It's sleep again, for me," Sarah said, "walking in gardens filled with orchids, walking through stained glass palaces, stately pleasure domes with caves of...."

"She seems to be really happy in her last days," Jonathan said. "I hope it lasts. The doctor thinks she'll just fade out, slowly."

"How long?"

"No one can tell. Maybe two days. Maybe two weeks."

"It's a great way to die, isn't it?"

"There's no great way to die," Jonathan said. "Those around you will suffer, even if you don't suffer yourself. But of course it's better to die quietly than to die roaring, as Captain Josh used to put it."

And then, one day, Sarah ceased to wake, though she seemed to remain semi-conscious in her sleep. Jonathan sat with her, hour after hour, holding her hand, and feeling the faint response to the pressure of his fingers. When he leaned over and kissed her cheek her lips seemed to move in the ghost of a smile. And, bit by bit he was coming to accept it, no longer, like St. Paul, "kicking against the pricks." During those last hours a sense of peace descended upon him. Perhaps, he thought, this, rather than her poetry, was really her final gift.

Then her breath began to rattle in her throat, coming lightly and slowly, slowly, perhaps not oftener than once a minute toward the end. Her flame of life was burning at the lowest possible flicker, so low that Jonathan felt for a pulse between breaths. And then — he couldn't be sure exactly when — the breath did not return, and the pulse was no longer there.

He sat for perhaps another hour, tears in his eyes, but healing in his heart, while dawn slowly spread its pearl-gray light over the rooftops. Then he went to call Judith, and to face calmly the years he must face alone.

Snipe Flight and Evening Light

He sits on basalt, an old man beside the sea, the sounding of the surf in his ears. Shafts of sunlight fall through slots in the cloud, pouring pools of liquid silver on the sea, illuminating distant islands and the channels that separate them. Sunlight walks across the water as the clouds move with currents of air, currents not of the same direction as those on the ground. He has seen the sea in many moods, sometimes with a wild sky pressing down, waves leaping like tigers to meet it, claws extended, light like sulphur. Now it is peace but not stillness; the drift of life continues in quietude.

Behind him on top of the cliff the brown bumble bees bend the clover blossoms as they have done every summer since bees and clover emerged together from the insects and plants that went before them. They seem not to have been harmed by the great destruction that humankind has visited upon the world in his lifetime. Creatures of the sea have been less fortunate, for the sea is now almost empty of the multitudes that crowded through its waters when he was a boy. The whales are gone, the seals, the larger fish. The sky itself is deadly, filled with menace. The waves now are all but lifeless, washing the rocks as they did in palaeozoic times, under the indifferent vault of heaven.

It was just here, from these very rocks, that he and his cousin Jimmie went diving into the green water more than half a century ago. How icy the water! Still is, he supposes, though he hasn't been into the waters of the Atlantic for more than twenty years. Jimmie and ... there was another boy from the city ... what was his name? Carl?

Carlos, that was it. He wonders where they are now, those old men who had been so quick and bright in that year of his first awakening.

Behind him the land rises by terraces through field and forest — just a narrow band of trees, actually, perhaps a quarter of a mile wide — to the Brigus Barrens and Colliers Ridge. When he was sixteen he'd wandered all over this countryside, the town, the gardens, the frog marsh, the woods, The Barrens, like he owned everything in sight. Not knowing exactly where he was, he'd come out of the trees into somebody's back garden, and then continue through their land to the road, as any neighbour might do, calling in a friendly way to a dog when it started barking; or he'd go up through their fields toward the screen of woodland, and then continue across the berry grounds, where the trees had been burned time and again in earlier centuries until trees would no longer grow there, but blueberries and kalmia and sheep laurel flourished. Somewhere along the way, as likely as not, he'd abandon his shoes, forget about them, and when he returned home his mother would scold him: "If you must go barefoot like a ten-year-old boy, for heaven's sake leave your shoes at home, not somewhere in the woods."

He smiles, remembering. In fact, he could retrace his route, and there the shoes would be, right on the trail. No one would touch anything they didn't own, even if they were very poor, even though some of the boys just up the hill in Marysvale had never owned a decent pair of shoes in their lives. You could leave anything, anywhere, and it would be there next day, or the day after.

Often he wandered alone, sometimes with his friend Jamie. Where was he now, Jamie Penchley, companion of his youth, who had settled in New Brunswick and never come home, even for a visit? And for a brief time, a marvellous interval between late summer and late spring, there had been the girl Virginia, and the utter magic of first love, as they did all things together — their school work, their wandering, their visits to "scoffs" and "times," the pleasures they shared with the other young people of the town.

And the separation — the break with Virginia had come when her family moved off to the city — people were always doing that — and what can youngsters do about it at fifteen or sixteen? They can't launch out on their own, so they are torn apart. Slowly, the tear had begun to heal. But he kept dreaming about her for two years or more ... three, perhaps ... and in all that time there was just the aching void, no real love in his life.

The merciful thing about old age, he thinks, is that you have lots of time to get used to it. If you were twenty-two, and suddenly couldn't ski any more, or hike up a mountain, it might seem like disaster, but when you're seventy-two, and have an arthritic knee, it doesn't seem to matter that your cross-country skis haven't been out of the basement this year. It won't matter if your grandson borrows your good ski boots and never returns them. You've gradually got used to slowing down. If you can still figure out the riddles in the MENSA ads, your mind must be alive, even if you can't remember the name of the professor who tried to teach you the inner meaning of elementary calculus.

Enjoying *this* year with its own possibilities, not measuring it against twenty years ago, is a trick you learn, with time. You may not be up to writing a computer programme for the horticultural society with its four-hundred-odd cultivars, but you can still design an iris bed that will be lovelier than last year's.

Indeed, he recalls, landscape design was something he hadn't even begun to discover before the age of sixty. Now he is surrounded by young women, all anxious to learn the secret, the hidden mystery, that makes his designs so successful, believing that he understands why a rock, a pond, a tree, placed just so, should combine to lift the spirits — and he does what he can — takes them to see successful designs, has them meditate on Japanese prints. Perhaps he should say, "All you need is to live another fifty years, and it will all seem so simple." Then, of course, they'd think him arrogant.

When you were young, the prospect of growing old seemed to be just about the saddest thing in the world, but as it happened, as old age slowly became a fact, you discovered there were compensations all along the line. Even when you finally faced the nearness of death at the end of this long road, it wouldn't prove to be so terrible after all, he believed — perhaps rather like badly-needed rest at the end of a long journey.

As you aged, people became more considerate. They offered to carry your things, made way for you, didn't expect you to keep up your end quite the same as they did when you were in your forties or fifties and finding life a mad scramble. The struggle eased with time, at least so long as your health remained good. Jonathan has a few complaints, it is true. His joints are stiff. He is always needing new glasses. He has trouble picking out information from the background noise that seems not to bother most younger people. He can no longer hear the top trilling notes of the golden-crowned kinglets, which delighted him on winter mornings long ago.

But there are compensations. He now has time for everything. One of the paradoxes of life is that as your remaining time on earth grows shorter, there is less and less hurry, more and more opportunity to savour the pure magic of the world, to pass it along, to help the younger ones — not so often the next generation as the one after it — to see the magic, to slow down just a little, perhaps enough to catch a glimpse of the riches that await those who are willing to take their time.

Mere physical things, too, have improved. There is far more decent wine to drink now than there ever was in his youth, when at best you might get a glass of sweet port or sherry or a taste of somebody's blueberry cordial. The quality has vastly improved, in step with the demand. Food is better too, at least here in North America. No more boiled mutton. No more plain fish chowders with only onions for flavouring. People here learned from Europe, and learned very quickly, it seems to him — in ten years? twenty? — to adopt the skills and knowledge of France, China, Mexico ... And music! Now it is everywhere, great music from the greatest composers, interpreted by the greatest performers, at the mere touch of a button. Who could have believed it possible fifty years ago when radio was primitive, and recordings were squeaky distortions overlaid with noise? Now there is great visual art, too, not just in distant museums and galleries, but everywhere. Included are closeup views of the outer planets and their moons, in beautiful colours, as fine as those of any terrestrial landscape, but having, in addition, the eerie quality of the utterly new. The electromagnetic field of the universe has come into human life, enriching it immensely. Can it be possible that this has happened just on the edge of extinction? He thinks not, though he has no proof.

There are other, human compensations. Younger people have actually come to him, looking for wisdom. He'd had this experience in his later years at the university, when young professors had sought his advice; but even that was less rewarding than the graduate students who came to him almost as though he were a sage, the guru of some great religious philosophy. They came, believing he had wisdom to impart. He hopes that he had a little in those days. He believes that he did. They, certainly, believed.

And love, the thread that runs so true, that ties the end and the beginning of life together, that makes it all worth while, love not just of the woman or child in your arms, not just of the trusted companion or the admired leader, but love also of the leaf that puts out its green tip on the bough, of the nudibranch that floats like a jewel in the water, of beetles that shine like fire, of the life that breathes through the whole world and blossoms in a million fanciful ways, a current of which you yourself are a part: O Love that will not let me go — ah yes! in a sense far deeper and truer than any cardinal of the one true church could ever suspect.

Can you explain love to someone who has never experienced it, as most, indeed, have not? And to explain the love of abstract beauty, a love that may begin in the desire of the flesh, but transcends it beyond all belief, is most difficult of all, as Plato well knew when he wrote *The Symposium*, and gave birth to the misconception called "Platonic love."

He lets his mind drift: across the generations, across the centuries ... Who knows what might have been here on this coast, in these seas, before us? There was more life in the world back then, before we had turned loose such powers of destruction. There was more to inspire awe and wonder. Sober old Captain Whitbourne, fishing admiral of St. John's in fifteen hundred and something, saw a mermaid swimming in the clear, cold water of the harbour. Whitbourne was no romancer. He reported just what he'd seen, and nothing more. But what was it? No seal or porpoise or other common sea creature looked anything like a mermaid. One of his crew, then, disguised for a joke? But surely anyone doing that would be running the risk of being shot with a musket ball?

"Maybe there really were mermaids back then," Sarah had suggested.

"Sarah! A creature half human and half fish?"

"Not exactly that, of course. But when the platypus was first discovered, wasn't it thought to be half otter and half duck?"

Sarah, with her pixie-like mind, combining deep doses of common sense, and even a scientific outlook, with romance and wild speculation. How lucky he'd been to spend most of his life with her, how sad that she is with him no longer. And yet ...

"There is a beauty at the goal of life,
A beauty growing since the world began ..."

He isn't quite sure of the quotation any more. From a childhood school book, he believes. Is it Archibald Lampman? Something, at any rate, that would never be included in a school book nowadays. He believes it, anyway.

He has been here in this place for a very long time, he and his ancestors — twelve or thirteen generations. His family was already living in Brigus when Champlain tried, and failed, to found a colony at Quebec. They had been there for at least two generations when Sir David Kirke, having banished Champlain from Canada, became the first royal governor of Newfoundland, appointed by King Charles of England. His ancestors' house was one of those destroyed when the French returned, and in a brief winter raid put Brigus to the torch. They had already rebuilt, on the site where his father's house still stood in his childhood, by the time King William got around to sending troops to protect the old colony.

Gradually, the afternoon wears into evening, and the snipes begin calling from the sky — that wild, wild call like spirits, the winnowing of their feathers through the air falling down to you out of the twilight. How many years have they been doing it in this same sky above this same shoreline?

The snipes, like the bees, will perhaps survive the human adventure, may outlive this incredible animal that has remade and nearly destroyed the earth. A brown vole runs through the grasses near his feet, pauses to look at him in wonder, as small mammals will sometimes do if a human is sitting rock-still. Brother vole, so much closer to us than the alien snipe. Will you go down with us, brother vole, into the dark, unknowing?

We the mammals now dominate the earth, inhabiting a space between extinctions, and when one day God wipes us from the page, there will be those who come after us, creatures beyond our wildest imaginings, perhaps at home in the depths of interstellar space, no Buck Rogers rockets, no star-ship *Enterprise*, none of that kid stuff that we played with for a while, but flying on thought-waves past all confines set down by Einstein's constants — or else as patient and immovable as redwoods, watching the dance of stars while the constellations slowly deform and regroup, and the earth rolls on, seeking some new encounter in its still mysterious destiny.